CHARLES BARBARA

My Lunatic Asylum

TRANSLATED AND WITH AN INTRODUCTION BY
BRIAN STABLEFORD

THIS IS A SNUGGLY BOOK

ISBN: 978-1-64525-038-8

My Lunatic Asylum

CHARLES BARBARA (1817-1866), the son of a luthier, became involved in Henry Murger's *Buveurs d'eau* group, before meeting Baudelaire and turning towards literature himself, though also playing the violin as an additional means of support. His first novel, *L'Assassinat du Pont-Rouge*, was first published as a serial in the *Revue de Paris*, before being published in book form in 1857. Other works include his collections *Histoires émouvantes* (1857) and *Mes Petites-Maisons* (1860), and the posthumously published novel *Mademoiselle de Sainte-Luce*.

BRIAN STABLEFORD'S scholarly work includes *New Atlantis: A Narrative History of Scientific Romance* (Wildside Press, 2016), *The Plurality of Imaginary Worlds: The Evolution of French roman scientifique* (Black Coat Press, 2017) and *Tales of Enchantment and Disenchantment: A History of Faerie* (Black Coat Press, 2019). In support of the latter projects he has translated more than a hundred volumes of *roman scientifique* and more than twenty volumes of *contes de fées* into English.

His recent fiction, in the genre of metaphysical fantasy, includes a trilogy of novels set in West Wales, consisting of *Spirits of the Vasty Deep* (2018), *The Insubstantial Pageant* (2018) and *The Truths of Darkness* (2019), published by Snuggly Books..

SNUGGLY BOOKS

Contents

Introduction

THE stories in this collection were first published in book form as *Mes Petites-Maisons* by Hachette in 1860. Of the six stories it contains, one, "Romanzoff," had originally been published before the 1848 Revolution, in the radical newspaper *Le Corsaire-Satan*, in 1846. The other five were all published under the Second Empire, "L'Homme qui nourissait des papillons" (tr. as "The Man Who Nourished Butterflies") in *L'Illustration* in 1853, "Les Sourds" (tr. as "The Deaf") in *Le Journal pour tous* in 1856, and the remaining three novellas in *La Revue française*, "Esquisse de la vie d'un virtuoso" (tr. as "Outline of the Life of a Virtuoso") in 1857, and "Le Major Whittington" and "Irma Gilquin," the latter as "Irma," in 1858.

Although the stories in the collection were initially published under two different reigns, they were all produced in an era of censorship, the rules of which they tested to some extent. The periodical in which "Romanzoff" was published had begun life in 1823 as *Le Corsaire*, subtitled a "*journal des spectacles, de la littérature, des arts et des modes*," the purpose of which supplementation was to emphasize that it was not a political paper, and, indeed, its primary purpose was to provide an organ for the fledgling Romantic Movement, many of whose leading lights it featured in its pages. The Movement and the paper could not, however, avoid an inherent ideological commitment to progressive ideas, and *Le Corsaire*'s radicalism was increased when it was briefly combined with *Le Satan*, an openly radical paper edited by Petrus Borel, during which interval, in 1844-47, Charles Barbara was a regular contributor, as he was to Arsène Houssaye's more heavily disguised *L'Artiste*.

After the 1848 revolution, when *Le Corsaire* changed hands, its radicalism was drastically transformed, and Barbara transferred his allegiance to other organs of the Romantic Movement, notably the *Revue française*, which flourished between 1855 and 1859 before being absorbed, like *L'Artiste*, by the more robust *Revue de Paris*. Like *Le Corsaire* and *L'Artiste*, the *Revue française* and the *Revue de Paris* were only tolerated because they were supposedly purely literary and artistic periodicals with no political involvement, but, like their predecessors, they espoused a progressive ideology that was only partly masked.

It is difficult for the modern reader to see anything very radical in these stories, but the egalitarian political ideas expressed incidentally by the eponymous Romanzoff were sailing very close to the wind, and the republication of the story in 1860 was even riskier than its original publication in 1846, which might be why it had not been included in Barbara's earlier shorter story collection, *Histoires émouvantes* (1857), issued before the Second Empire censors began to relax slightly. There is some surprise in the fact that "Le Major Whittington" did not provoke suppression in 1858, when those censors were still so active that they muzzled literary expression for the entire decade of the 1850s. The Church no longer had as much influence on the censors as it had had before the 1848 Revolution, but the defiantly atheistic conclusion of the story was nevertheless highly provocative for its time, even if read sarcastically, as it is doubtless intended to be.

"Romanzoff" can now be seen as an interesting precursor of the genre of crime fiction, to which the author made several other early contributions, and "Major Whittington" as an early example of *roman scientifique*, and in both cases, their enterprising digression into those nascent genres can be regarded, in part, as a response to a climate of censorship that encouraged obliquity as a strategy for approaching questions that could not be addressed straightforwardly.

Modern readers, considering the title that Barbara gave the collection and reading the dedication might assume that it is a collection of "case study stories" of mental aberration, akin to William Gilbert's near-contemporary *Shirley Hall Asylum* (1863), or Edmond Thiaudière's later *Trois amours singulières* (1886; tr. as *Singular Amours*), and it does have some affinities with those volumes, but it is much more various, and only "L'Homme qui nourissait des papillons" really qualifies as an early example of "case study fiction," albeit an interesting one, especially in its touches of surrealism.

The implication that Romanzoff might be the victim of a pathological obsession, tacked on to the end of his story, is clearly not serious and is only suggested as an "explanation" of his career to deflect attention from the possible inference that his criminality is actually a species of political rebellion against unjust tyranny.

Major Whittington, far from being insane, could almost be seen as a model of a superior sanity, which is only treated flippantly by the story's laconic narrative voice in order to mask the seriousness of the implicit arguments of the narrative. While the author obviously does not see the futuristic world that forms the background to the story as a utopia, the features that he questions, overtly and covertly, are merely exaggerated features of the world in which he lived; it is notable that Major Whittington is conspicuously sympathetic to the poet to whom that society, like the author's, offers very cold comfort. All three main characters in "Irma Gilquin," like the protagonist of "Esquisse de la vie d'un virtuoso," are subjected to searching psychological analysis by the narrative voices of their stories, but none of them is ripe for confinement in a lunatic asylum, even the hapless virtuoso, whose manifest madness is self-contained, understandable, and beyond the attainment of any possible therapy. It is not a coincidence that the career of the virtuoso in question overlaps that of the author to a sufficient extent to suggest a certain self-accusation and personal regret in its analysis of his ills and their causes. Seen as a whole, the collection is not an examination of mental pathologies so much as an exploration of the human condition, illustrated by inspection of idiosyncratic features that are by no means all flaws. The story labeled a "*post-face*" [appendix] is an entirely apt allegory, in which the deafness of the characters undermines their lack of bad intentions, generating ironically troublesome misunderstandings.

It was entirely natural that the writers of the French Romantic Movement should be powerfully attracted to the discoveries and hypotheses of the fledgling science of psychology, because the very heart of their philosophy and endeavor was to provide a more honest and more searching account of the role played by emotion and delusion in human affairs, and to examine aspects of human behavior and motivation in a more accurate and sympathetic fashion than their consideration in the framework of a stubborn absolutist morality permitted. In that regard, there is no conflict between Romanticism and Naturalism, and Charles Barbara's work, like the work of such immediate predecessors as Honoré de Balzac, George Sand and Gustave Flaubert, illustrates the extent to which the two movements were aspects of the same crusade. "Irma Gilquin," in particular, can be seen as a member of an interesting cluster of texts that undertook to re-examine and re-evaluate female psychology. Although it was published shortly after the masterpiece of the cluster, Flaubert's *Madame Bovary* (1856), it is not an imitative exercise, any more than other texts nowadays seen as foundation-stones of French Naturalism, including the Goncourt brothers' *Soeur Philomène* (1861) and Émile Zola's *Thérèse Raquin* (1868), but an endeavor motivated by the same curiosity. It is primarily anomalous within the cluster because of the peculiar extremism of the author's sympathy for Irma—an idiosyncrasy common to many of his depictions of women, including the oddly-unnamed and self-effacing heroine of "Esquisse de la vie d'un virtuoso."

✳

Louis-Charles Barbara was born in Orléans in 1817, the son of a maker of musical instruments whose character was apparent tyrannical, and against whose pressure he rebelled—although his schooling in the violin was later to prove useful in providing the crumbs of a living in periods when his writing did not make him enough money to support him. Like the protagonist of "Esquisse de la vie d'un virtuoso" Barbara reluctantly turned performer with voice and violin when circumstances were tough, as they frequently were in a turbulent era.

Barbara was still a child when the French Romantic Movement first got under way. Arguably, by the time he joined it, it had already passed its heyday, even before it ran into the economic reefs associated with the upheavals of the 1848 Revolution and its aftermath. He arrived in the heart of "Bohemian" Paris, however, in time to be parodied in Henry Murger's *Scènes de la vie de Bohème* (1847-1849) as "Carolus Barbemuche," and to form firm friendships with Charles Baudelaire and "Champfleury" (Jules Fleury-Husson). Barbara edited two overtly political periodicals in his native Orléans during the brief interval of the Second Republic, *Le*

Démocrate and *Le Constitution*, but that career was cut abruptly short by the consequences of Louis Napoléon Bonaparte's *coup-d'état*. He returned to Paris and continued writing throughout the 1850s, when the literary marketplace was under its greatest pressure from the censors.

Having shared Baudelaire's enthusiasm for the work of Edgar Poe, making his own translation of "The Murders in the Rue Morgue," Barbara's ventures into crime fiction are entirely understandable, and his first novel, serialized in the *Revue de Paris* before being thoroughly revised for its initial book publication in Belgium by the then-exiled Pierre-Jules Hetzel in 1855, *L'Assassinat du Pont-Rouge*, owed a considerable debt to Poe. Antedating Paul Féval's *Jean Diable* and the early detective stories of Émile Gaboriau by some years, *L'Assassinat du Pont-Rouge* warrants consideration as the first significant work of the French genre that was gradually transformed into the *roman policier*, and "Romanzoff" further emphasizes that priority in its depiction of the methodical way in which agents of the Sûreté track and eventually capture the mysterious forger. Barbara's earlier collection of short stories, *Histoires émouvantes* (1857), which followed closely on the heels of the Poe collection *Histoires extraordinires* (1856), from the same publisher, also echoes Poe's work in more respects than its imitative title.

"Le Major Whittington" similarly has affinities with one of the major aspects of Poe's endeavor, but its more obvious affinities are with two works published in the *Revue de Paris*, of which Barbara was undoubtedly a reader even in his teens: X. B. Saintine's novella "Histoire d'une civilisation antédiluvienne" (1830; tr. as "The Story of an Antediluvian Civilization") and Charles Nodier's two-part narrative, "Hurlubleu grand Manifafa d'Hurlubière ou la perfectibilité" and "Léviathan le long Archikan des Patagons de l'île savante ou la perfectibilité" (1833; collectively translated as "Perfectibility.") Both those stories include sarcastic depictions of societies transformed by enormous technological advances, which overlap in many respects the advancements anticipated in "Le Major Whittington." Barbara's consideration of that transformation is more even-handed in its laconic satire, and in its treatment of automata it is closer in spirit to Edmond Thiaudière's "Mistress Little" (tr. as "Mrs. Little") in *Trois amours singulières*, which might well have taken some inspiration from it. Like the other works Barbara published in 1858 and thereafter, it demonstrates that his influences were wide and his ambitions greater than merely recycling ideas borrowed from Poe.

It is now easy to see that the works assembled in the present collection are historically important, but they were initially published in difficult circumstances when the possibility of commercial success was remote. The collection was swiftly followed by *Les Orages de la vie* [The Storms of Life] (1860), labeled *première série* and containing two novellas, "Thérèse Lemajeur" and "Madeleine Lorin," but no other volumes appeared. Barbara's subsequent works were less innovative, his primary market thereafter being the somewhat downmarket and carefully diplomatic *Journal pour tous*, where his second and third novels were serialized. Although censorship under the Second Empire eased in the 1860s, in which decade the genres of crime fiction and *roman scientifique* both made vast strides in France in other hands, Barbara was only able to publish a handful of further stories in that decade, although several of them are substantial in length; his last novel *Mademoiselle de Saint-Luce* (1864 in *Le Journal pour tous*) only achieved book publication posthumously in 1868, the same year in which his fourth and last collection of short stories and novellas, *Un Cas de conscience, Anne-Marie, L'Herboriste, L'Accordeur, L'Officier d'infanterie de marine* was published.

In 1858 Barbara had produced a dramatic adaptation of *L'Assassinat du Pont-Rouge,* which was produced at the Théâtre de la Gaité and enjoyed some success, but he was not able to follow that up either. In 1861 he married and had two children, in spite of his awkward financial circumstances, but his wife and daughter died in a typhoid epidemic in 1866 and the consequent mental distress led to his internment in a lunatic asylum, where he swiftly committed suicide by jumping out of a window—an end which can be compared and contrasted, with a certain macabre irony, with the conclusion of "Esquisse de la vie d'un virtuoso," penned ten years earlier—and, indeed, with the entire ambiance of *Mes petites-maisons.*

Although his career lost impetus after the publication of *Mes petites-maisons,* which shows him at his very best, and *Les Orages de la vie,* Barbara was undoubtedly an important and innovative writer, who might well have been able to do more spectacular work had he not been working in the censor's shadow and under pressure following his marriage to produce work slanted to perceived public taste. Like Champfleury and Charles Asselineau, he has tended to be pigeon-holed by critics and historians as a "friend of Baudelaire," but it would be grossly unfair if his work were to be eclipsed even by such a vast shadow. He was a fine writer, heroic in his tribulations, and he left behind some first-rate works, including the bulk of the present collection.

This translation was made from the copy of the 1860 edition of *Mes petites-maisons* reproduced on the Bibliothèque Nationale's *gallica* website.

—Brian Stableford

My Lunatic Asylum

Dedication of Mes Petites-Maisons

To Doctor Baillarger[1]

MONSIEUR,

I have had the great pleasure of attending your lecture of mental illnesses. A powerful attraction attached my attention to it; enlightenment springs from it that, by virtue of its brightness, is sometimes cruel. Under the charm of your speech, one trembles for one's neighbor, and is full of anguish for oneself. Who would dare to flatter themselves, after having heard you, that they incessantly escape the mirages of hallucination? "There

---

1 Jules Baillarger (1809-1890) was a neurologist who studied under the pioneer of psychiatry Jean-Étienne Esquirol, and worked at the Charenton mental hospital as a student. He subsequently obtained a post at the Salpêtrière before becoming the director of a sanitarium. His psychiatric studies included a strong interest in hallucinations, on which subject he published an important book in 1844, and the hypnagogic state intermediate between sleep and wakefulness; he also produced one of the earliest descriptions of what is nowadays known as bipolar disorder.

is no superior mind," Seneca wrote,[1] "that does not buckle somewhere." More exclusive still, you clearly give the understanding that, in the lot of every human being, the seed of madness is rarely absent. I am inclined to believe you, Monsieur; all the madmen are not in Bicêtre, nor all the madwomen at the Salpêtrière; it does not seem to me to be too paradoxical to advance that, on the immense surface of our planet, the lunatics that are locked up are neither the sickest not the least interesting.

From there, Monsieur, to offering you this book there was only a small step. The figures whom these sketches have the object of putting in relief can, with a more or less well-founded entitlement, lay moral claim to an abode in the strange Babel in which your penetration and your science are exercised; how can I avoid the dream and resist the temptation of placing them under your benevolent patronage?

Deign, Monsieur, to accept this dedication, which, on my part, is certainly the pledge of the most sincere admiration as well as the most profound sympathy.

Charles Barbara
Paris, June 1860.

---

1 Author's reference: "*De tranquillitate animi.*" The dialogue in question concerns the state of mind of one Serenus, beset by chronic anxiety and disgust with life, and the possibility of restoring his calm of mind.

Outline of the Life of a Virtuoso

Part One

Now, divine air . . . Is it not strange that sheep's
guts should hale souls out of men's bodies?
Shakespeare.[1]

AN old man glides through the streets, going past
the houses like a shadow. The curve that his tall
stature describes makes him resemble a fragment of an
arch standing in the midst of ruins. Long gray curls
fall over his neck; wrinkles furrow his forehead with
profound arabesques; his pale face is full of holes and
angles; fogs fill the orbits of his eyes; the projection of
his large nose shades the lips, where a smile of bewilderment reigns perpetually. His head hanging down,
his limbs heavy, dreaming about who knows what, he
is not marching but dragging himself along. Under his

---

1 *Much Ado About Nothing*, Act 2 scene 3. The line is often mis-
rendered, incorrectly substituting "hail" for "hale," because modern usage has abandoned that formulation of a word nowadays
spelled "haul."

wretched garments of disparate colors, scarcely ample enough for his thinness, he dissimulates as best he can the instruments of his living: a violin and a bow.

A shadow of a shadow, a woman is following him at a distance. Someone unfortunate to that degree is rarely solitary. Bowed down like him, by a similar funereal melancholy, equally poorly clad, she watches him with a gaze in which compassion and tenderness burn. One would try in vain to avoid the annoyance of astonishment. What appearance is there, in fact, that that poor man, curbed by the weight of a nameless misery, reduced to wandering relentlessly from one quarter to another, from one crossroads to another, was once, at the Conservatoire imperial de musique, one of the brilliant pupils of Rodolphe Kreutzer?[1]

A few details of his origin and his debut in life are essential to an understanding of the episode after which his reason remained buried under errors. Antoine Ferret, his father, vegetated in the provinces. He was a skillful maker of musical instruments, whose infatuation for the art of music, and for its artistes, was fanatical. One fact gives its measure. In a house with scarcely sufficient space to contain his instruments, his tools, his child and his wife, he imposed the inconvenience on himself of an elegant room that was rarely vacant. The names of all the celebrated musicians who had occupied it by turns would be very surprising. It is only a matter of characterizing a worthy man in whom enthusiasm and vanity stifled any preoccupation of material interest.

---

1 Rodolphe Kreutzer (1766-1831) was a violin professor at the Conservatoire from 1795 until 1826.

No anticipation, however menacing, could have cured him of his disinterest. Before renouncing the honor of receiving artistes in his house, the pleasure of seeing them at his table, of chatting to them, or hearing them, of procuring here and there a lesson for his son, he would have ruined himself blindly twenty times over.

Ostentation was not the least of his faults. Passionate, violent and vindictive, of an intractable humor, incapable of enduring contradiction outside of his dealings with artistes, and above all, of an intemperance of language with no possible restraint, he never ceased, by virtue of his abrupt manners, his trenchant tone and his causticity, to provoke hostilities.

The triumphant hour of his day sounded in the evening, when, at the back of his obscure shop, he had an audience, not counting his wife and child, of two or three people who were listening to him open-mouthed. Not content with rambling on about music, relating anecdotes about the celebrities of his acquaintance, which he arranged in his own fashion and dressed in fabulous colors, he passed his clients in review, peppering some with sarcasms and expressing himself on the count of others in the most wounding manner, without any reserve, and without ever appearing to care about the prejudice that his indiscretion might cause him. One would have sworn that his clientele was dependent on him and not him on his clientele. He would not consent, at any price, to repair the instrument of a man who contradicted his opinions, whereas he hastened to make one for a flattering fiddler from whom he never received a centime. Finally, incredibly, even in moments of distress, he would break an advantageous bargain under the singular pretext that the buyer was not worthy of the merchandise.

The things from which he did not think of taking vanity were exactly those in which his true merits resided. Except for his son, who witnessed it, the following adventure was absolutely unknown. One afternoon, the worthy man was in his shop when a young stranger suddenly came in. It was divinable, from the dust on his garments that he had descended from a vehicle. His eyes were haggard, his features distraught. He was holding a violin-case. In that case, the back of which was broken, was an instrument that was scarcely in a better condition.

Under the strings that the bridge no longer sustained, between the end and the fingerboard, one of the extremities of the sound-post appeared, which had traversed the table from side to side and occasioned a wound of distressing irregularity. That spectacle was all the sadder because the form of the violin had an adorable suavity and its color and bright gleam. There was no doubt that it was an expensive instrument.

While the instrument-maker examined the wound curiously, the stranger recounted the accident in a tearful voice. As a safety measure he had put the instrument on top of his luggage, so that nothing heavy would weigh upon it. An unfortunate hazard had determined that the vehicle was overloaded. As it went at a gallop under the arch of the Post Office, the keystone of the vault had weighed brutally on the violin and had literally crushed it. The young man added that he was a

Spaniard, that he had come to seek his fortune in Paris, that he had no other resources than those he expected of his instrument, and that he was doomed if, as he foresaw, the misfortune that had overtaken his violin was irreparable.

Ferret had had time to measure the extent of the damage. Raising his head and fixing his glaucous eyes on the young artiste, he told him to have courage, that the harm was not without remedy, and that he only asked for four or five days to prove it.

The Spaniard, in his doubt and his impatience, found the days that followed as long as centuries. Well before the agreed hour, he irrupted into the instrument-maker's house like a madman, out of breath.

"Well?" he demanded, in an extinct voice.

Ferret's response was to open a box and reveal an intact instrument. The young man seized it. For a few moments he was mute with amazement.

"You're making fun of me!" he cried, suddenly. "This violin isn't mine!"

"Are you sure?" asked the instrument-maker, ironically.

"No, no, it's not my violin," the foreigner repeated, increasingly perplexed.

Antoine had, in fact, worked a miracle of sorts. He had not limited himself to reconnecting the lips of the wound; he had also collected the numerous splinters of wood, the majority as thin as needles, and had stuck them back in place scrupulously; and that mosaic work, which required no less patience than art, had succeeded so perfectly that it was impossible even for a forewarned eye to recognize the place where the table had been fractured.

The foreigner's joy was boundless "Where I thought that I would only find, at the most, a skillful work-man," he said, "I have encountered a great artist." He took five louis from his purse. "Believe in the shame I experience," he added, "in only being able to offer you this miserable sum. Not to mention my admiration, I would gladly give you a thousand francs, for you have saved my life."

"Keep your money," the violin-maker replied, tran-quilly. "You need it for the voyage."

The Spaniard opened his eyes wide and seemed to be searching for the meaning of that refusal.

"If you absolutely want to please me," Ferret said, "stay here for a week. You can lodge with me and eat at my table. I only ask that you give some advice to my son . . ."

That action revealed his most intimate depths.

But how little the only offspring of that man re-sembled his father! Likening him to a sick branch of a vigorous tree, the image would be only too well-founded. Only a brain troubled by fever could have been deluded. A child comes into the world with the seed of flowers and fruits that he will one day bear; with rare exceptions, he announces in the beginning the class of men to which he will belong. Will, energy and pas-sion are not acquired; they hide in young breasts like fire in the entrails of a mountain, always betrayed by smoke and flashes. Young Ferret, closely observed, was nothing but an extinct volcano, so to speak. His weakness, nonchalance and inertia were such that, even at school, where he had languished for three or four years, his comrades had inflicted him unanimously with the sad and characteristic nickname of Ferret-la-guenille.[1] His passivity was deplorable; one could only draw the saddest horoscope therefrom.

The father only saw that as a matter for self-congratulation. A slave himself to his despotic instincts; he employed his son as a sculptor makes a model with wax ready for any form and any imprint; he molded him in his own image, inoculating him with his ideas and prejudices, as well as his ambitious aspirations, if not his temperament and his passions. The child, with his soft and spongy nature, cradled in the rumor of absurd legends, struck incessantly with the spectacle of a disinterest akin to disorder, was impregnated with the most false ideas of life, the most erroneous opinions about art, and an inconsiderate enthusiasm for artistes: all things that took root within him and prospered there, so to speak, like couch-grass in rich soil. He even succeeded, under the empire of threat and in fear of being beaten, in acquiring an artificial vivacity that his father mistook for activity.

Scarcely was he able to whistle the seven notes of the scale than a violin was hastily placed in his hands. Although his thin and tall stature, his long arms and his slender, supple, agile fingers favored him in the work of that instrument, he had a weak and idle brain, a

---

1 Literally a *guenille* is a rag, but the term can be applied familiarly to anything worthless.

slowness of conception that rendered him inapt to concentration and profound study. He had, in addition, the irreparable misfortune to become, at the age of ten years, the dupe of an aged music teacher who, devoted to ignorance and routine, taught him absolutely nothing. Thus, when, by agitating his fingers and the bow, he could execute difficult concertos, after a fashion, he was still incapable of deciphering the most insignificant sonatas.

For want of knowledge, the father was not alarmed. Far from grasping what was abnormal about that development, he witnessed it with folded arms, without the appearance of any anxiety. The good man, who lived in a fever, imagined that he was thinking because he was incessantly dreaming. Apart from the resolution to abstract his son from the condition of orchestra musician, he only had confused ideas about anything else; for instance, he put on the same level the performer and the composer, confounding the virtuoso with the interpreter of genius, and was quite convinced, in his vague, ill-defined ambition, that he had only to want it, and to ruin himself, for his son to become a Mozart.

Gradually, the day came when the debilitated young man was directed to Paris and interned at the Conservatoire. Initially an object of universal benevolence, at the same time he amazed the professors by an astonishing facility; he saddened them by virtue of his detestable education, and received from all mouths the advice to take the elementary classes. He did, in fact, slip into them obediently, only to escape almost immediately, ashamed of seeing himself confounded with children who mocked his tall stature and his blunders. The dexterity of his fingers gained therefrom; his progress on the instrument was one of the most rapid.

After some six years of stubborn toil, admitted to compete, he carried off the second prize right away. The following year's proof was a veritable triumph for him. And yet, the first prize that he was awarded on that occasion, in spite of his notorious incapacity as a musician, caused him scarcely half an hour of intoxication. He required no more in order to comprehend that than a passage from a letter from his father: *I shall only mention your prize as a memoir; what would fulfill the ambition of someone else can only be a prelude for my son, a beginning of fortunate presage.*

In spite of distance and the change of environment, he had not stopped living under the exclusive influence of paternal reveries. More than that; as he had grown up, his first impressions, like characters inscribed in the bark of trees, had developed proportionately and strengthened in his soul. Age had only modified him in the dimension of volume. Deep down, he was the same creature, possessing nothing of his own, a veritable machine for conserving the improvisations, paradoxes and divagations of whoever imposed on him, and appearing only to prove the adversaries of innate ideas right a hundred times over. From which it can be rigorously concluded that the dream that gradually took possession of him, the pride to which his poor soul strove to give shelter, the fever that made him progressively more ill, and the conviction that ended up invading him that he had the making of a powerful individuality, were, in sum, nothing but the dream, the pride, the malady and the conviction of the old violin-maker. How, after that, could he have been excited by a success that his father claimed to envisage as a simple school prize?

In any case, whether he was obeying his own inspiration or a foreign impulse does not matter. What matters above all is that an obsession, whether it is innate or borrowed, can ignite, even in a debilitated individual, fever, tenacity, energy and violence. In that regard, Ferret became an exemplary figure. The idea of succeeding in something of which he had as yet only a vague sketch in his mind triumphed incessantly over his weakness and nonchalance, communicating the strength to subject himself, from morning until evening, without missing a single day, to the most terrible toil. In any art, superiority is only acquired at the price of heroic perseverance.

One is struck with amazement at the extent of the labor to which a man must subject himself simply to play a violin a little better than the common run of violinists. As soon as he pursues an irreproachable accuracy, produces sounds that have the volume, roundness and flexibility of a human voice, and imports into their execution the degree of artistry that creates belief in a natural artistry rather than the result of long and fatiguing travail, life fails his ambition.

Perfection is a siren who can no longer count her dupes and victims. One rows toward her with passion and fury, one gets closer, but just as one flatters oneself that one is about to seize her, she dives, and reappears on the distant horizon. Her demands with regard to the instrumentalist have no known limit. The duration of the exercises that she imposes is endless, and the monotony of those exercises would trouble the most solid mind—which is to say that it is difficult to comprehend how a man endowed with some intelligence can resign himself to turning the mill that is known as working on an instrument. To that painful and repulsive task, comparable to the punishment of Sisyphus, the son of the violin-maker devoted himself body and soul. For nearly fifteen years, ripened in isolation, deprived of all joys, he thus had to spend, in pursuit of a goal that was in reality trivial, as much patience, obstinacy, skill and courage as would have been necessary to assure a position ten times over in any other career. Doubts, disappointments, dolors and disgusts, far from making him flinch or recoil, were only as many spurs that multiplied his ardor tenfold and hastened his course.

Profusion and lack of order had gradually thrown his father into difficulty; it was only at the price of his own existence that the old man could sustain his son henceforth. Even by imposing ever greater privations on himself, he only succeeded in granting him a pension that was quite insufficient. Apart from the fact that the poor fellow lodged under the eaves and nourished himself poorly, he was always dressed like a pauper. He was not even impatient with that lack of wellbeing. He did not suffer overmuch from it; he got used to it, and even ended up taking pleasure in it. That naïve insouciance, developed by education, took on the proportions of an incurable chronic malady. One could already recognize in him one of those distracted, preoccupied individuals who, incapable of taking care of themselves, need to be governed like children all their life.

That was not enough. It seemed that the father had resolved to remedy the evil by excess. Stubborn in a frightful negligence, with his eyes fixed on the mirages of the future, he responded to his son, in whom he thought he remarked symptoms of lassitude:

"My predisposition to suspicion is doubtless deceiving me in this instance. I cannot suppose that you ever know discouragement. Recall to memory incessantly what I have repeated to you so many times, that it is necessary not to earn a living too soon and thus consent to make an art into a métier. The future is cloudless for the man who toils; to acquire talent is to amass certain wealth. Are you weary of suffering already? You are not my son, then. I abandon the roses of existence to you, and keep the thorns for myself. The miseries that are heaped on me are only known to you in part. Your mother is ill; the business is not going well, the figure of our debts rises every day, our house is cracking in all parts and ruination is threatened. Afterwards? I shall be reduced to alms, of which I won't collect a sou. My body will be fodder for worms before I permit you to become an orchestra scraper. Engrave this in your memory, and dig the graver in until it traverses you: I have a thousand outrages to avenge; you will make a name for yourself or I shall die of shame and despair."

At a word from his father, Ferret was precipitated into a pit. Letters of that sort tore his heart gratuitously, since the task that he had accepted, which was beyond his strength, already possessed him as narrowly as a vocation.

By virtue of one of those hazards that create belief in predestination, a young woman had come to lodge in a mansard neighboring his own. Without relatives or ties of any sort, always alone, she only lived on the condition of working all day and part of the night. Analyzing her features coldly, she was not beautiful, and yet the candor, tenderness and chastity that illuminated her face rendered her as agreeable to behold as if she had been beautiful. Of medium height, well-constituted, of solid health, she bore on her forehead, in her eyes, on her lips, in her gait and in her attitudes, the gentle and affectionate serenity of those mothers whose patience and solicitude nothing can weary. At the same time as the need to devote herself, to suffer for others, drew her imperiously toward the weak, true effluences emanated from her of an irresistibly attractive virtue.

Between her and Ferret, who was several years her junior, there were neither agreements nor oaths. They scarcely exchanged a few words. Their liaison, founded on an identity of nature utterly mysterious for both of them, formed as simply as that between drops of water on the same slope. In their angelic candor, an intimate fraternity sufficed for their contentment. While Ferret, his head lost in the clouds, worked doggedly, his companion, in whom intuition substituted for intelligence, who only knew how to love and act, watched over him as over a child, and enveloped him with a sort of order and an ineffable peace: an embalmed atmosphere in which he breathed as if in paradise.

That gentle, beneficent regime imprinted on the weeks and the months the rapid flight of days. Ferret did not feel happiness; that peaceful household life was his real vocation; it had increasingly powerful charms for him and gradually enlaced him with invisible bonds that slid all the way to the depths of his heart and took root there. Sometimes he shivered and seemed to be emerging from a dream. After a few days of feverish meditation, remorse invaded his soul and deprived him of all repose. Thinking of his father, who was sleeping on ardent coals, and his mother, exhausted by labor and privation, he reproached as the equivalent of a crime the joy of being loved, and in his impotence to triumph over his scruples, he resolved to break off an association whose sweetness revolted his conscience.

It is impossible to describe how painful the struggle was. It was a matter of breaking, one by one, all the sensitive strings that were vibrating within him, and falling back into an isolation that delightful and im-perishable memories rendered horrible henceforth. Nevertheless, he consummated the sacrifice. Without saying a word, without consulting his companion, who divined everything but made a semblance of see-ing nothing, he rented another mansard, moved there covertly, and, his heart swollen by chagrin and his eyes full of tears, brutally quit a friend who was veritably the marrow of his bones, the blood of his veins, the light of his eyes and the soul of his soul.

Under various formulae, life has been compared endlessly to a cup of bitterness mingled with a little honey. The image, appropriate to the life of the greater number, was quite inappropriate to the existence of Ferret. It could be said that his lips only dipped into the cup to find a beverage that was increasingly bitter. Thus, while still at grips with the black sorrow caused him by the sacrifice that he had just accomplished, he was struck in the heart by a new one, terrible and crushing.

Too occupied with his own impressions to care about the sensibility of others, his father addressed to him unsparingly a cry of despair:

"My son, your mother is dying. She is asking, in her delirium, for the supreme consolation of seeing you and embracing you. It's frightful, my son—curse implacable fortune with me—but it isn't permissible for you to respond to that dying wish. A voyage would not only distract you from your work, it would also absorb a part of the feeble resources that I send you in order to live. Refrain, therefore, from weakness. Your mother is subject to the common law. Limit yourself to expressing, in a letter, sentiments that will attenuate the horrors of her agony. In the meantime, my dear son, be bronze before dolor, hold firm; let nothing stop you; work! My enemies are rejoicing; their number increases incessantly. I would be incapable of struggling for much longer were it not for the hope I have in you."

That misfortune was foreseen. Nevertheless, Ferret nearly lost his reason in consequence. He was only submissive to his father materially, as it were; by contrast, his mother, whose cares, tenderness and sublime devotion he never recalled without emotion, had all of his love. That mother was himself; without her, life would no longer have any charm. He wept as if to lose his eyes; the violence of chagrin crushed and broke his heart.

"My mother!" he cried, in a fit of derangement. "I shall never see you again! I shall never seen you again, and you will never know how I've suffered from your long martyrdom. How much I loved you, how much I love you! But I was only working for you; my unique ambition was to give you at least a few days of joy. Oh, my mother, with my dream, you're taking away my strength and my courage!"

The wound was one of those that never heal. An enervating sorrow penetrated his soul and increased its languor and disorder sensibly. Only the paternal influence on him, an influence that nothing was capable of weakening, could hinder that deterioration. At the memory of the old man, he soon returned to himself and redoubled his obstinacy; his energy turned to rage. He no longer found enough hours in the day; he paled further for part of the night over a few books on composition that he had in his hands.

In his feverish persistence, haggard, so to speak, he was reminiscent of a man walking through a wood, hastening under the empire of frightful visions. If he sometimes stopped, it was to pray and weep. Gripped by inexpressible anguish at the sentiment of his tottering strength and the time that was fleeting, he forgot himself completely and cried: "O my God, let me at least live long enough for his glory and consolation!"

In the midst of those days darkened by mourning, distress pressed the old man with a pitiless ardor. The affinity of similar things is well-known; disaster summons disaster as, in another order of things, a magnetized steeple attracts lightning. In sum, he had not recovered from the stupor into which the death of his wife had plunged him when he saw himself constrained, by the poor state of his affairs, to request clemency from his creditors. The letter in which he announced that latest catastrophe to his son was full of imprecations against what he called destiny. Without mentioning his unfortunate tendency only to see enemies everywhere, he had to be placed in the number of those men who do not want causes to produce effects. It is sometimes the case that we accumulate deliberately, without being aware of it, a series of faults that result in miseries that overwhelm us, and we spend the rest of our days cursing Providence or fortune.

In fact, most of the time, is one not tempted to believe that destiny and fatality are only words created at will, either to caress our pride or to render our vanity invulnerable?

Ferret *père* at least had this about him that was touching, that all vicissitudes imaginable could not succeed in shaking his virtue. "After all," he cried, "my ruination will not lead to my dishonor. A pure conscience remains to me in the depths of the abyss; even my enemies, whatever they say or do, cannot prevent justice being rendered to me, and I am proclaimed unanimously as a perfectly honest man. You do not have to blush, then. My disaster, far from bringing you down, ought to multiply your vigor a hundredfold. In your place, I would be electrified; I would have genius! Let my misfortune serve as your stepping stone, I ask for nothing more. What does my life matter! A name, make a name! If, for one day, or one hour, I can see the joy of my enemies turn to torture, all my chagrin will be effaced, and I shall die intoxicated. But great God, hurry; don't lose a second! Toil and anxieties have worn out my body; strength is abandoning me; my old age is only hanging by a thread, and that thread you have in your hand."

It is difficult to understand how Ferret, so weak of mind, so tender by nature, did not succumb under the effort of shocks that might have broken the soul of the most robust of men. To tell the truth, the bitter old man, always beside him in spite of the distance, sustained him, encouraged him, communicated a kind of fever to him and galvanized him. A dream—the only thing to which he could attach any value, in view of the people and the circumstances of the environment in which he had been brought up—still stimulated the straw fire that paternal ambition alimented in his breast. It had gradually organized and determined the individuality that he wanted to be.

His goal inevitably formed a perfect equation with the sum of intelligence, sentiment and knowledge that he possessed. To be a virtuoso, to swell the phalanx of brilliant soloists who, like comets, produce a surprising glare and vanish without leaving a trace: that, in reality, was his ambition. For want of elevated musical faculties, a bizarre, deregulated imagination had germinated within him and developed there by reason of the weakness of his brain. While he slowly paraded the bow over the strings all day long, beating trills, or carried out more difficult exercises, his mind, momentarily as troubled as the gaze following the movement of the hands on a clock-face, suddenly produced extravagant fantasies that he mistook for as many marvelous creations.

Not content to hear them, he executed them in thought in a theater, in the midst of a hall glittering with light, where an avid crowd was pressed as if to crack the walls. In the presence of that auditorium, of which the women were the soul, he enjoyed, in anticipation, the most splendid triumph. To his delight, it was said that he owed his skill to nature itself. His accuracy, his vigor, his agility and his conceptions were incomparable. He wanted even more. The setting and the pantomime were among his preoccupations. His exterior ought to be one of the essential parts of his personality.

He was tall and thin, with broad shoulders, a face with large features, strongly emphasized; long blond hair floated over his neck; toil, privations, anxieties and grief, in hollowing out his pale face, had imprinted a strange and mysterious character thereon. He saw himself as he wanted to appear. The public shivered merely at the appearance of that singular individual. People asked with terror where he came from. His execution was only more extraordinary and gripping. People cried magic and miracle. In human memory, no such prodigy had yet been seen.

He was no longer an ordinary being composed of flesh and bone, set in motion by human springs; he was a curious and moving phenomenon, a monster escaped from the world of visions to strike, dazzle seduce, magnetize and fanaticize humans. The increasing admiration that he provoked became delirium; the din of applause filled his ears; he was recalled twenty times and saluted with transport; he heard himself proclaimed the greatest of artistes; he fainted under a deluge of flowers. To complete the intoxication, the newspapers, in enthusiastic articles, were unanimous in exalting his genius and bearing his glory to the ends of the earth. In addition, his mysterious existence lent itself to absurd fables, which finished making him a legendary individual prematurely.

His name was on all lips, his image on all walls; each of his days counted a new triumph. From that moment on, fortune had nothing but caresses for him. A rain of gold encumbered his mansard and that mansard was transformed into a magnificent town house where a series of scenes succeeded one another as touching as they were romantic. He was not content to extract his father from need and assure his independence; he disinterested all the old man's creditors integrally. The tribunal pronounced his rehabilitation and the judges, in that circumstance accorded to the son eulogies that rebounded on the father and made his probity resplendent. Ferret wept warm tears in consequence.

Then, in the place where his mother reposed, the eternal object of his amour and his regrets, a sumptuous tomb was erected. Afterwards, alms ran through his hands like water from an inexhaustible spring; he helped all unfortunates, and had it said of him that he was not only a great artiste but a man of great heart.

Who has not had those generous dreams at least once in his life?

Finally, after active research, he enjoyed the profound, supreme happiness of rediscovering the gentle and lovable woman whose cares and tenderness he had once repaid with abandonment, the devoted and discreet friend whom he had loved, whom he still loved, whom he would always love; and his existence, sheltered henceforth from the uncertainties of hazard, defended in all directions by honor and consideration, went by peacefully in the midst of a beautiful and joyous family.

In hours of truce he was already measuring with an impatient mind the few years still necessary for his integral development. The days began to appear to him to be strangely long. It was taking him a long time to shed his shadow and finally claim that fortune pursued through so many ruins.

At intervals, however, the wind brought him rumors to which he lent an ear with increasing anxiety. Gradually, he was agitated by the vague, painful presentiments that sometimes oppress on the eve of a catastrophe, and finally, by his prostration and his bleak attitudes, he resembled a man overwhelmed by the apprehension of a new deluge or the end of the world.

The cause of that was simple. An Italian violinist, whose reputation had never ceased growing for some time, was threatening to fall upon Paris. In Florence, Venice, Rome, Naples and twenty other cities he had been awarded enthusiastic, delirious ovations. After having resisted the most splendid offers for a long time, he had finally decided to leave Italy. His excursion to Germany resembled a triumphal march. There was more fuss over his itinerary than that of a traveling sovereign. Cities greeted him like a prophet. In Vienna, particularly, he had excited a mad intoxication; in the number of his most ardent admirers, the artistes themselves were ranked; a medal had been struck in his honor, and new fashions bore his name. He quit Vienna for Prague, Prague for Dresden, Dresden for Berlin, Berlin for Warsaw. Everywhere he unleashed fanaticism and fury. Several times the rumor had run around that he was heading for Paris, but, perhaps by calculation, he had always deceived the hope of the Parisian dilettanti. First he was to traverse Holland and sojourn in Frankfurt.[1]

The newspapers never wearied of citing his name; every time they added a more sonorous and more bombastic epithet. His personality had taken on colossal proportions in the public gaze, and the curiosity he inspired, kept awake by the fanfares of publicity, had attained a rare intensity. The papers and the posters finally announced his arrival in Paris and his first concert at the Opéra.

Ferret was direly worried by all these diplomatic maneuvers and had observed with alarm that the virtuoso had conquered, inflamed and fanaticized Paris before even setting foot there. What was said about his works, his execution, his appearance, his life, and his foreign mores ended up filling him with fear, since it

---

1 The description and biography of this violinist are clearly based on the unique career of Niccolo Paganini (1782-1840), who toured most of the major European cities between 1828 and 1831, but left Paris until last, causing a sensation everywhere, his abnormally long fingers allowing him to play notes that no one else could.

would not have taken much for him to recognize in all those details, if not his entire life, at least the realization of his own dream. His head was in ferment, like that of a man with a fever; his faculties already so weak, lost all elasticity; he could not sleep, could not work, was no longer alive.

But for one last hope, perhaps he would have gone mad immediately. Estimating that the Italian was employing diplomacy and cunning for want of being at the height of the admiration he inspired, he took pleasure in thinking that the appreciations were false, or at least singularly stained by exaggeration. In his isolation, he had lacked the opportunity to observe that very often there is no great artiste, not to say great man, devoid of a good deal of charlatanism.

Nevertheless, his anguish was to have a terminus. The moment had come for him to be edified regarding the value of a menacing rival. Although he was ill, devoured by fever, exhausted, and in profound destitution, he dragged himself through the streets in the middle of the day and, at all risks, dared to mingle with a queue that was already considerable. The invisible attraction of the spectacle and the fear of being excluded from it inspired a superhuman courage in him, temporarily consolidating his debilitated organism.

Alarming words circulating from mouth to mouth added to his martyrdom. The administration, pressed by demands, had judged it appropriate to convert half of the ground floor into stalls; one could therefore presume that a large part of the crowd besieging the doors would be refused entry. Tickets for boxes put up for auction had attained a figure that surpassed plausibility. There was no example of a man who had ever excited such a violent curiosity in minds.

The hours, for poor Ferret, were as many years of torture. A cold sweat inundated his forehead, as happens when the heart is about to fail. Fortunately, night fell and the offices were opened. He had no sooner slipped into the enclosure than he collapsed on a bench, where he remained for a long time, stunned, crushed and annihilated.

The hall was overflowing with spectators and buzzing like a hive of a hundred million bees. A signal resounded. At the same time as the leader of the orchestra came to sit down at the lectern, the curtain was raised; a profound silence fell and the *tutti* burst forth. Ferret shivered and raised his head. He was distraught.

The man who appeared on the stage had the effect on him of an apparition. He was thin and livid, and his frail legs seemed to buckle under the weight of a marvelously expressive head. On his broad and square forehead you might have seen with a little complaisance, the rudiments of horns. Beneath the perfect arch of his eyebrows, dark eyes scintillated, from which emanated a truly fascinating charm. His enormous nose, rounded at the tip, betrayed energetic passions, and the rictus of his thin lips no less malice than intelligence. A robust chin terminated the triangular face, defended, in a way, by ample ears, the projection of which pierced the brown hair that fell profusely over the shoulders. Between the lip and the chin, a silky tuft flourished, comparable to a cast shadow or even a large black fly.

44

Finally, in his jacket, long arms played at their ease, to which powerful hands were attached, armed with slender fingers like the feet of grasshoppers. In his exterior there were, at the same time, genius, mystery, cunning, strength, flexibility and the dexterity of a clown. From that mixture resulted an extraordinary figure, which participated in those of satanic nocturnal evocations. Hoffmann himself, in the hours of his most abnormal hallucinations, had never dreamed, glimpsed or described a stranger, more fantastic or more troubling individual.

Had that man been created for the violin or the violin for that man? It seemed that the instrument adhered to his neck and that the man and the violin were only one. The ancients had the centaur; a new expression would have been required to render that adherence, that fusion of a man with an instrument. Appearances unusual to that degree already had the virtue of troubling and imposing. It is necessary to add that the prestige of a glory as resounding as that of the most illustrious captains, and a life black with romantic horrors, ignited around his person a kind of supernatural phosphorescence. One expected prodigies. The immense majority, immediately seduced, were rapidly penetrated by influences that predisposed them to exaggerate their own impressions. A boundless success was certain if the execution of the artiste responded in any measure to that expectation.

He ranked precisely among the number of rare men who can do more than their reputation promises. The crowd was to find him even greater than it hoped. As soon as the first notes, it was enraptured, and it had not listened to twenty bars when it could only contain its enthusiasm with difficulty.

Through the chaos of the introduction, the virtuoso slid here and there a few phrases that sparkled with spontaneity, and the gleam of firelight in darkness. Like the tempest, he advanced escorted by lightning. From one second to the next his stature became taller, he radiated more vivid splendors, until the moment when he launched himself, in all his majesty, into the confusion of a vigorous crescendo, like a god from the milieu of the clouds.

In a grave, pure, powerful, incomparable voice, he intoned a song of supreme breadth. It was a veritable magic. Under the mysterious, irresistible influence of sonorous waves, everything was transformed, magnified and idealized: the enclosure, the auditorium, the artiste, the occasion. The enraptured crowd, involuntarily strayed into the half-light of the vast circuits of a temple, witnessed the celebration of some redoubtable mystery. One might have thought that Michelangelo's Moses, shaking off his age-old lethargy, had been suddenly animated under his marble to shake the pillars and the vaults with the words of a sublime canticle.

That unique voice, struggling with the crushing mass of the orchestra and dominating it, plunged into rapture and ecstasy. One breathed the impression with the air, after a fashion. From the depths of the soul to the epidermis, the listener shuddered; sweat moistened faces, tears rose to eyes, all breasts suffocated with sobs. Drowned in the penumbra of a box, the creator of that inspired song wept himself, like a child. No spectacle more solemn, more imposing, had ever inclined heads; no prayer more majestic had ever resounded in human ears; no faith more vivid and more ardent had ever made hearts beat and transported them. By the amplitude and the penetrating ardor of his execution, the virtuoso, attaining unknown, inaccessible heights, stifled in the least enthusiastic minds any desire for examination and discussion, tamed the most stubborn resistances, and subjugated the most rebellious wills.

It arrived that the crowd, in which one would not have recognized two similar natures, no longer had any but one body, one intelligence, one heart and one soul in order to believe, to weep and to be enthused. Happy in its servitude, it surrendered itself with an absolute abandonment to the enchanter who charmed them at his whim, moved them, electrified them and possessed them ever more narrowly.

With a spontaneous impulse, the entire audience stood up and testified to its stupor, its emotion and its admiration with applause similar to the thunder of a battle, by the reiterated recall of the artiste, and by acclamations of an indescribable violence. During each entr'acte the same effervescence bubbled up from the floor to the amphitheater, into the boxes, all the way to the corridors. It required nothing less than the promise of new sensations to temper that sort of fever and put an end to the clamors of enthusiasm.

The monster reappeared. One might have feared that he could only remain below himself. He surpassed himself. Emotions of an entirely different order were already stirring souls. If he had the power to evoke somber images, to generate fear, to provoke tears, he possessed to an equal degree of intensity the art of driving away melancholy. With the wave of a wand, the crowd, still under the empire of a sentiment of magical terror, suddenly found itself in Venice, in mid-carnival. The scene was populated by a multicolored multitude.

From the four corners of the horizon, floury pierrots came running, harlequins with black faces, doctors with large spectacles, braggarts with wooden swords, charlatans in red robes, masked with all forms and all colors. Nothing could be seen but humps, false noses, deformed calves, extravagant collarets, pointed hats, and gigantic plumes. Grave men fled as far as their legs could carry them. Jokes, puns, quips and epigrams mordant enough to draw blood escaped from that crowd like apple-juice from a watering-can. The unexpected face of a police commissaire excited formidable boos; while one sprinkled him with soot and another with flour, a third made him drink a bitter sauce.

Nothing was sacred for that mob of grotesques who, struck with vertigo, were all chattering, dancing, pirouetting, singing and bursting into laughter at once. At every note the spectacle was enriched by some new element. In the center of a joyful circle, a mime was grimacing, a clown turning somersaults, a funambulist dancing on a rope, an acrobat juggling with daggers. There was miracle after miracle. The serenade had its turn. What did the magical execution of the musician have to say? Trills, arpeggios, chromatic scales, pizzicato, staccato, harmonic sounds of an inexpressible perfection, profusely entangled, streamed from his fingers as from those of a fay.

The sounds, multiplied like the atoms of a cloud of dust, while continuing to evoke jubilant phantasmagorias, sometimes depicted long and rapid rockets that flew through the air to fall back in cascades and clusters, or even more sparkling, like a firework display radiant beneath a black sky.[1] And thus, graduating his effects with a marvelous artistry, incessantly increasing his vivacity, verve, impetuosity and excess, the magician, without stirring any more than a rock, his eyes sparkling, his lips pleated by a diabolical smile, heaped prodigy upon prodigy and rose up to vertiginous heights where only a madman could think of following him.

Compared with the hurricane that was unleashed in the hall, the transports of the debut were only a distant storm. A veritable frenzy took possession of the crowd. The sublime artiste was recalled endlessly, without taking account of his lassitude. The frenetic stamping of feet, insensate cries, impetuous surges, comparable to thunderbolts, never ceased to shake the walls of the theater. A band of fanatics could not have been excited with more vehemence and fury by its idol. The women, bewildered, were literally tearing the flowers from their hair and their belts in order to throw them. Surely, in

---

1 There is an untranslatable play on words in this sentence, the word *fusée* [literally, rocket], also being the French term for a sequence of musical notes usually described in English more prosaically, as a "run."

human memory, no virtuoso, no actor, no victorious general, had ever excited such delirium, or had ever had his head circled by a more dazzling crown. It was, to say everything in a single phrase, the masterpiece of triumph, a triumph such that it is impossible to imagine a greater one.

And it would be unjust only to see here a summary of the purely personal impressions or reverie of a visionary. The newspapers of the epoch, and the biographies, will testify, if necessary, that this analysis, far from exaggerating the picturesque proportions of the individual, remains, for want of sufficient merit, well beneath the truth. He produced shortly thereafter, with his military concerto and his variations entitled *Le Streghe*,[1] an even more surprising impression. He could be exalted with impunity, without exposing another to a disappointment.

He was not unaware, in any case, of artifices capable of striking the imagination and magnifying the idea that people had of him. People in the métier recognized that he did not disdain to have recourse to the tricks of charlatanry in order to heighten his merit as a performer. Not to mention that the strangeness of his external appearance, his immured life and his systematic mutism gave rise to stories that he allowed to run around for a long time and to be believed. Like fogs that magnify appearances, the mystery with which he enveloped himself gave him superhuman proportions, multiplying a hundredfold the desire to hear him,

---

1 Paganini's *Le Streghe* (1813) [The Witches' Dance] is a series of variations on a theme from a ballet by Salvatore Vigano.

and adding as much to the power and magic of his execution.

Later, he became the victim of his own tactic. When, sated with glory and fortune, he wanted to descend from the clouds and become a simple mortal again, to live life like everyone else, he ran into invincible prejudices. At one time the animosity took on a character to the odious degree that he could do no less than protest energetically. At his plea, this note appeared in the newspapers:

> *He is eager to thank the respectable public for the benevolent welcome he has received; but he believes at the same time that the slanderous rumors spread by the vulgar necessitate on his part an authentic and formal declaration. He protests, therefore, as much in the interest to his reputation and honor as that of the truth: never at any time and in any place, under any government whatsoever, has he been constrained for any reason to an existence different from that which befits a free man, an honorable citizen and a faithful observer of laws. That is what results from the testimony of all the authorities under the protection of which he has been able to live freely and with honor for him, for his family and for the art that procures him the advantage of appearing at present before a public as knowledgeable and as appreciative as that of Venice.*

That appeal to common sense remained without effect. The vulgar were obstinate in seeing in him a fantastic murderer who had been jaundiced in dungeons and who owed his marvelous talent to a pact with the devil. Even scholars seemed jealous to participate in the error and to increase it. A physiological report was read in a full session of the Académie on his physical structure and his fatal aptitudes, absolutely as if it were a matter of a fossil or a biped of an unknown and recently discovered species.

Whatever he did, the man could not succeed in having himself removed from the category of phenomena. Even his death gave rise to the strangest incidents. On the strength of rumors that vain efforts were made to belie, he was refused a sepulcher and his heirs were obliged to engage in a long lawsuit with the Church in order to obtain a Christian tomb for him.[1] In the meantime, an audacious businessman did not fear to offer thirty thousand francs for the cadaver, in order to exhibit it to the eyes of Europe like an embalmed monster . . .

---

1 The Church refused Paganini a Christian burial in his native Genoa because of rumors regarding his diabolism; after much controversy and argument he was not buried until 1876 in Parma, thirty-six years after his death.

Part Two

Nature is cruel; she only cherishes, among her
children, those that are robust; the weak she
abandons, and she even furnishes them with
arms that they direct against themselves.
                                                Hoffmann.

Sometimes, in slumber, it seems that one has the lightness of a bird, that one is lifted from the earth involuntarily all the way to the stars, and that one falls back
abruptly with the weight of an aerolith. One experiences something analogous in descending from regions
of enthusiasm to the side of a wretch in whom everything conspires with dementia. A single phrase would
suffice for his funeral oration: "Mediocre minds have
no destiny," if one did not sometimes see a mediocre
mind pass for great and a great mind not to be reputed,
precisely because of that destiny. It is a point as important as being born at the right moment.

A man matures for ten, fifteen, twenty, forty years
in solitude; he exhausts his energy and his intelligence
there, accumulating marvel after marvel. His consciousness finally informs him that he finally has a right to
that for which he is ambitious, a little glory; he emerges
from the shadows. Ought he not to remain there, since
he only escapes to experience a mortal disappointment,
to recognize that his discoveries are already old, already
applied everywhere and fallen into the public domain
long ago? He has no more reason to live; in everything
that meets his eyes he reads a sentence of death; impo-

tence and despair whip him until his final hour, and he will die under torture.

All things considered, was that not precisely Ferret's story? He came too late. His presentiments had not deceived him. At the same time as he found himself preceded on a route that he thought new, he observed with terror that he had been aiming at a goal that the Italian artist surpassed by a hundred cubits. No image can give the measure of his disappointment. Coup after coup, without respite, he was subject to a series of sensations diametrically opposed to those of the crowd. He was moved, undoubtedly, but like someone whose heart is being crushed, the membranes of his brain being torn apart. His dream flew away as the sun is extinguished at the advent of night.

The hopes in exchange for which he had offered his life were like those images that only interrupt the blue of the horizon in order to seduce pale pilgrims and drive them to despair. Whichever way he turned his eyes, he only perceived misery and shame moving through ruins. His father was dying in indigence; his mother had no tomb; the beloved of his soul, forever lost to him, was withering in isolation. The hurrahs, the stamping feet, the enthusiasm of the public were as many sledgehammer blows staving in his chest and bruising his head. He suffered to the point of no longer being able to feel pain.

His mind was disturbed; bewilderment paralyzed his reason; his body became an inert mass. The passage of a thunderbolt would not have made more frightful ravages within him. In the darkness of his thought, one supreme ambition was dominant, but an inextinguishable, immeasurable ambition: that of no longer seeing the light, of no longer sensing his heart beating, of reposing forever in the immobility of annihilation.

A veritable wreck, he abandoned himself to the crowd, the waves of which, in their multiple oscillations, shoved him outside. Under the peristyle, scarcely had the human sheaves that held him upright come apart than he folded up and lost consciousness. People hastened around him. He opened his eyes. A few people helped him get up again.

His distraught features and the incoherent words that he stammered gave rise to the supposition that he no longer had his reason. At least the mildness of his eyes did not announce a dangerous madman. He was, in any case, poorly dressed. Insensibly, solitude and shadow enveloped him. Then, his head bowed, his eyelids half-closed, he headed at an unsteady pace toward his quarter, and groped his way to his mansard.

An intense fever made his teeth chatter and threw him into delirium. The most energetic remedies were impotent at first to master the violence of the illness. Under the excitation of cerebral transports, he bounded on his bed like a reptile in a cage of fire. At other times, to see him writhe, one might have thought that his entrails were being devoured by flames.

Not content to rip up all the objects within arm's reach, he tried several times to climb out of his window.[1] It required nothing less than perpetual surveil-

1 It would probably be mistaken to see this episode as a precognition; it is more likely that, when the author actually committed suicide in this manner, for want of the constant surveillance that preserves Ferret, he had this story and its analysis in mind.

lance to preserve him from suicide. In less than a week he aged frightfully; his emaciated features were tinted with cadaverous hues, and the species of consumption by which he was attacked progressed to the point that the physician despaired of his days.

An officious neighbor took charge of writing to his father. His naïve and unambiguous letter only produced a new misfortune. On learning, contrary to all prevision, that his son was dying, the old violin-maker, attained in the place where what remained of his life was concentrated, fell backwards. All that was picked up was an old man who was rambling, and whose limbs were struck by an incurable paralysis. Ferret had nothing for which to hope in that direction. However, his malady was prolonged, and the poor people who had helped, finally penetrated by the sentiment of their insufficiency, began to find the weight heavy of a charity in which they were suffering without relieving the other.

At the moment when they were deliberating having him transported to a hospice, a woman—an old woman that no one knew—suddenly arrived, with the melancholy and discreet air of a phantom, to install herself beside his bed. Her calm, her reserve, her face full of forbearance and the character of authority that she bore in her person, so to speak, caused them to allow her to act without even daring to ask her questions.

The assiduous care of that providential nurse, who was not to be separated from him henceforth, extracted him insensibly from death. Humanely speaking, would it not have been better if he had not come back? The poor man only recovered his strength for his mind and his eyes to be afflicted with the most lamentable of spectacles. His brain was irreparably wounded. From the depths of his memory, overturned by dolor, nothing any longer surfaced but a vague and bitter sentiment of impotence, which, as it increased, plunged him into a melancholy ever more profound and extinguished the glimmers of reason that the malady had left him.

We know, however, that nature is cruel; she only cherishes among her children, those that are robust; the weak she abandons, and she even furnishes them with arms that they direct against themselves.

An energetic man, in such an occurrence, would have reacted quickly against the poisoned needles of disenchantment. While accusing his star, either he would have persevered bravely, at the risk of being only a reflection, or he would have given a rare example of a hero who confesses that he has taken a false route and boldly changes career.

A virtuoso, in any case, only occupies a rank in the arts such that one cannot be jealous of another without falling. With rare exceptions, it turns out that his domain is not that of music, and that his place can only be at the summit of the pyramid at the base of which acrobats and players with goblets strive. Too often, in brief, his ambition seems to consist, not of moving people, but of making them say: "How clever that fellow is! With what grace he tumbles!" Like those pretended great actors who do not want anyone around them but understudies, and sacrifice theater itself to their frightful and disastrous soloist ego, he is hardly ever anything but a devouring and sterile personality.

Corelli, Fiorillo, Pugnani and Viotti have founded schools and left works that assured them of a durable name. Paganini, on the contrary, because he only had an admirable eccentricity, is already no more than a memory. They live, and he, who seemed bound to make them all forgotten, who "sounded so well," reposes forever under the epitaph: *Periit sonitu.*[1]

But in addition to the fact that Ferret only had a borrowed energy, feverish and unhealthy, a sum of forces too narrow not to be rapidly exhausted, that he imagined seeing in every grain of sand an embryonic mountain, that he exaggerated beyond measure the importance of an unfortunate coincidence, he also lacked the faculties necessary to change the direction of a development that was, in sum, entirely instinctive. From the day when he fell from the height of his unique dream, he had infallibly to deem himself lost forever.

One cannot take a step in life without bumping into one of those martyrs of which art seems to have the privilege. Because they lack a powerful will, an elevated judgment or philosophy, a great disappointment or a violent chagrin is sufficient to knock them down and bar their route. They are complaisant in their despair; they do not cease to magnify and envenom their wounds, until the hour when the malady takes possession of them or their reason is troubled, when too often, finally, if they do not have recourse to sui-

---

1 The complete line from Psalm 9 is *Periit memoria eorum cum sonitu* , translated in the A.V. as "their memorial shall perish with them" although *sonitu* means "noise" or "rumor" rather than "memorial"—making the author's adaptation more apt.

cide, they fall by degrees into an abyss of misery and abjection.

Like those who are their own mortal enemies, Ferret now had a destiny. Impotent to dominate causes that had been produced fortuitously, he was even more so to ward off a chain of rational and fatal consequences. Under the empire of a depression heavier than a world, his shoulders buckled, his brain was numbed and his memories became increasingly confused. At the same time as he forgot his father, he seemed not even to notice the guardian angel who had cared for him during his illness. Melancholy and taciturn, he accepted mechanically the tutelage of that woman and allowed her to govern him completely. Eating the same bread, sleeping in adjacent rooms, they offered an example, edifying for some and damnable for others, of those associations in which, to the perpetual inertia of one, the other strives to oppose a perpetual activity, an inalterable patience and a sublime abnegation.

Although he was dead to any preoccupation with art, and the mere contact of his instrument caused him a disagreeable frisson, Ferret, at the insistence of his friend, did not recoil before the difficulties of collaboration.

It did not seem that the old violin-maker had been poorly inspired when he feared for his son the harsh condition that nevertheless became his only resource. According to musicians themselves, the orchestra, which sometimes fills the soul of the listener with the most exquisite and vivid enjoyments, is only an inexhaustible source of annoyances for those who compose it. Every day that God makes, from six o'clock until midnight, for an insufficient salary, it is necessary for weeks, months, years, entire centuries, that they execute and hear the same chords, the same accompaniments, the same modulations, the same good, mediocre or absolutely negligible works. A sadder, ruder, more repugnant, more horrible task is certainly inconceivable. So, even the best-endowed enter the orchestra full of an ardor that does not take long to be extinguished, to give way to a profound disgust—hence the singular remark that everyone likes music, except perhaps for the people whose profession it is to execute it.

They are precisely the victims of exercises that demand on their part neither intellectual effort nor the expense of sentiment, which even exclude those things by leaving all their faculties dormant. Their essential merit, in sum, consists of being perfect automata. An exemplary orchestra is a sort of labyrinth at the center of which an inflexible despot is enthroned, a pitiless dragon who, possessed himself by the demon of art, pretends, *per fas et nefas*,[1] to enslave the others. In the number of artistes who come to arrange themselves under him, the most estimable are incontestably those who have enough intelligence and tact to comprehend that they ought only to be slaves, supple and docile cogs, and that it belongs to the despotic dragon alone to have a will, and intelligence and a soul.

Does the assertion seem paradoxical or exorbitant? Here is the score for a new symphony, signed by an unknown name. Expect that the interpreters, even

---

1 "Through right and wrong."

the most skillful, will recoil before the difficulties of execution, declaring the work baroque, unintelligible and incapable of execution. They will travesty a few passages, shrug their shoulders and tax the author with ineptitude, if they do not immediately proclaim him a madman. That is for the best. The light will thus remain eternally under the bushel. Composers do not have, like painters, sculptors and poets, the resource of putting themselves in communication with the public without the help of intermediaries.

Miraculously, the leader of the orchestra arrives—a man worthy of that title, of course. The man of genius is still a man, perhaps—and it is seen all too frequently— mediocre; the veritable leader of an orchestra must of necessity be a superior man. He will be learned, a great musician, endowed with a high intelligence, but that is not enough; it is also necessary—a rare thing!—for him to have a powerful will, an imperturbable perseverance, that he be a character. His flair sometimes outstrips in finesse that of a savage. A glance is sufficient for him to sense the value of a work. He takes possession of it; he has no repose until he has read it, analyzed it and performed a sort of autopsy, a dissection of it.

His joy knows no bounds if fortune has put some-thing beautiful in his hand. Fever mixes with it, and then passion. He studies it incessantly, he can no longer let go of it. At every step there are unexpected discover-ies, new marvels, some sublime passage whose meaning escaped him at first, and his admiration increases, and again and again he sees the masterpiece, plays it over and over in his head, until he finally knows even the slightest details of it, and hears it sounding within him incessantly, and carries it fully armed in his brain. He is obsessed by it, he dreams it, he suffers from it, and he will only be delivered from it on the day when he succeeds in making all his impressions and all his enthusiasm pass into the soul of others. But how far he is from that glorious day!

Tenacious, iniquitous prejudices, rebellious wills, will all be obstacles for him, and the patience of a saint, the energy of a heroic apostle, will not be too much to reduce the deaf and stubborn resistance of people who are obstinate in closing their eyes and blocking their ears. He might as well be struggling against a band of fanatics. What will become of him, in fact, in the midst of that mocking, undisciplined mob, ever ready to revolt? He will be less than nothing, he will give the sickening spectacle of a general mocked, whistled and dismissed by his army, unless, in his conviction, he has the courage and the strength to be a redoubtable autocrat, determined to vanquish even at the expense of his life.

Before him, in an amphitheater, his orchestra develops; to the left and the right are the violins; further away the violas, then the cellos and double-basses; then the wind instruments; then the brass section, then the cymbals. After a little summary advice and the indication of the tempo, the signal for the attack is given. All obey, but negligently; the debut lacks precision; it is necessary to recommence. They recommence, but only to do it more poorly. A general would break his sword; the leader of the orchestra holds firm. He knows that it is easier to reckon with the resistance of a crowd of skeptics than the patience of a convinced mind. Strong in his conviction, he allows talk and murmurs, and pursues his task imperturbably. He reprimands one, shouts at another, appeals to the conscience of one and the amity of another; he flatters, pleads, begs, is irritated, is angry, is exhausted, multiplies repetitions, wears away ill will, until the orchestra, war-weary, impatient to finish, begs for mercy.

Meanwhile, here and there, through the work, a few flashes gleam. Suspicion penetrates the hearts of the musicians. They are astonished, and involuntarily, are captivated and become attentive. From the chaos that gradually clears, the general idea emerges, takes on color and sparkle. The moment has come to study the details, to make the movements precise, to take account of the slightest nuances, to regulate the accompaniments, to indicate the meaning of the melody, to give it the expression that belongs to it, to graduate and clarify the crescendo.

And it is at this point that one can understand the necessarily automatic role of the orchestra musician. Take the violinists, for example. Suppose that there are twenty, and that they all have sentiment; a melody, some passage, presents itself; each of them will render, express and accentuate that melody, that passage, with the sentiment appropriate to him. Where one will inflate the sound, another will diminish it; where this one judges that a slight acceleration is necessary, that one will slow down, and so on: a frightful mess that will only end when the twenty various sentiments dissolve into the sentiment of one alone, that of the leader of the orchestra.

Finally, by dint of shrewdness, diplomacy, patience, even violence, the latter has succeeded in disciplining his soldiers, in making them as many blindly docile springs. He has before his eyes a single sheaf, a single body, a single instrument, a marvelous organ that he can play in accordance with his whim. That orchestra is no longer a club of a hundred individuals tyrannized by different opinions; it is a kind of Briareus, with a hundred arms and a hundred mouths, full of soul, full of fire, full of vigor. Those hundred voices are no longer any but a single voice with the power of an admirably endowed man, a great artiste, an interpreter of genius. One might believe that one were seeing him at work in that bust of the Chevalier Gluck, whose incandescent mask once illuminated an entire corner of the Musée français.[1]

At his lectern, like the Pythoness on her tripod, he is ready to render oracles. His gesture is imperious; his eyes are ablaze, his forehead is inspired. He dominates everyone with his despotic will; he animates everything with his powerful breath, his passion and his vehemence. He speaks, sings, inflates his voice to the proportions of thunder and deflates it to a murmur, draws away, approaches, takes pleasure in melancholy stories, intones hymns full of gaiety, causes splendid landscapes to surge forth before the eyes, shows himself to be alternately

---

1 Presumably the oft-replicated bust of Christoph Gluck made in 1775 by Jean-Antoine Houdon (1741-1828).

tender and passionate, violent and terrible, awakens in the soul a thousand dormant memories, spreads by turns joy, melancholy, fear and intoxication.

And the transported public bursts into frenetic applause, and the musicians themselves, drawn by enthusiasm, do not take long to participate in it. Does it not seem that it is especially for that man that a poet has said: "You equal the intelligence that you comprehend."

It was not, however, under the orders of such a skillful, demanding and intractable leader that Ferret found himself enlisted. One might have hoped that he would succeed in maintaining himself there. He would at least have escaped the hazards of an errant and miserable life. Unfortunately, no human power was capable of warding off the consequences of his deplorable education. For having missed his studies of scales and having constantly refused to make music in ensemble, he was much inferior to the rabble of mediocre players whose routine makes them as many intrepid and imperturbable soldiers. If he extracted beautiful sounds, if he played accurately, with a perfect ease, on the other hand, he was such a poor musician that not a week went by when, even in the middle of a solo, he did not commit some monstrous blunder.

He had to deal with essentially mocking comrades, pitiless for the errors of others and perpetually in pursuit of distractions to fill in the void in their souls. Ambition, around which people flock in servile fashion when it succeeds, becomes a sort of irredeemable crime in human eyes when it fails. How could people whom Ferret had disquieted for a long time with his ambitious dreams show him any mercy? Had he not, furthermore, a mildness, a weakness, a natural distraction that predestined him to the role of victim?

His neighbors amused themselves with him; he was selected as the target of incessant mockery; every day he was the victim of some new trick, and gradually became a plaything, not only of all his comrades, but of the trivial personnel of the theater; and the persecutions multiplied by virtue of the very disdain that they seemed to inspire in him. The truth was that, living within himself, absorbed in an unfathomable sorrow, he did not perceive the comedies to which his credulity gave rise. Sometimes, he even forgot where he was and stopped short in the middle of a passage, bowed his head and wept. His dejection, the streams of tears that flowed from his eyes, far from exciting compassion, accumulated grievances against him. For entire months he did not cease to be the object of the sharpest recriminations. Finally, he was judged incorrigible; he was dismissed.

The check was decisive. It happens that prejudice drives roots within us so profound that it became impossible to dislodge them. If a man, for example, is prejudged as lacking in merit and tries to make another depart from that judgment, it will not be sufficient for him to acquire the merit; it will be necessary that he possess it to a degree capable of wounding the sight, and more. But in his depression, Ferret did not even think of raising his eyes to his comrades. He allowed himself stupidly to be crushed.

From the Théâtre Feydeau he passed to a secondary orchestra, soon to succumb there to the weight of his insufficiency and his detestable reputation. From that moment on he went from one fall to another, and from one affront to another. His existence became comparable to the day, which, after noon, never ceases to decrease until it is extinguished in the dusk, and then in the night. Incapable of defending himself, even when accused unjustly, he wandered from theater to theater without succeeding and settling in any. Such much defamation ended up dishonoring him in the end, so that he could no longer obtain a place even in an orchestra of the lowest order.

It was not upon him, moreover, that the burden of a situation weighed of which he seemed to have no consciousness. It was upon his companion that the miscalculations, embarrassments, uncertainties and dolors of their communal existence fell, as into a gulf. At first she had caressed the hope of seeing him cured, but she had understood at length that the poor man's condition stemmed from incurable lesions. Gradually, she had made a duty out of thinking, foreseeing and acting for him and playing the role of a good angel around his premature decrepitude.

At least he obeyed her with an exemplary docility. She said to him: "Get up," and he got up; "go here, or there," and he went; "sit down and eat," and he sat down and ate. Thus, when the exigencies of their life rendered staying in Paris impossible henceforth, she indicated to him a theatrical agency where he signed, blindly, an engagement to direct a vaudeville orchestra in the provinces. In the beginning, he was remembered at intervals, but so many years passed that he was completely forgotten.

The accumulated details of that phase of his life show him always at odds with the same misfortunes. Sometimes in one place, sometimes in another, living in miserable circumstances here, giving a few lessons there, he did not succeed in acclimatizing himself to any sky. Chased from city to city, incapable of creating a stable position, he wandered through France for a long time, and was finally brought back to Paris by miseries similar to those that had driven him away from it.

In his increasing aversion for his instrument, he had only touched it when constrained to do so. His marvelous facility had given way to the most gauche and maladroit fashions. He only drew sounds from it of dubious accuracy, devoid of strength and purity; his limbs already had the rigidity of an old man's; his fingers, once so alert and so docile, now seemed numb and refused to obey. Of a brilliant pupil, who had taken nearly fifteen years to attain perfection, an equal number of years of idleness, neglect and nonchalance had gradually made a kind of village fiddler.

However, the level of his poverty rose as that of his talent declined. One would have dreaded recognizing him. He had reached the state of decrepitude in which a man no longer inspires any interest. Scarcely was his name pronounced, scarcely was he perceived, than doors closed of their own accord, as it were. The responsibility of his companion became increasingly heavy. She had exhausted herself in superfluous efforts to stop him on the slope of the abyss to the bottom of which he was sliding. At odds with the most dolorous perplexities, she had to recognize herself fortunate to succeed in having him admitted to the musicians of a dance band.

It was a vain descent. Sad to relate, for that new métier, in which he was to complete his extinction, he had neither the necessary means nor sufficient strength. He found himself mingled with men who, not content to abuse his weakness without any reserve, used the pretext of his slightest omissions immediately to proclaim him absolutely incapable. Just as he had gone from theater to theater, he went from barrière to barrière, fell from guinguette to guinguette, and arrived, after several years in that degrading state, to seeing himself excluded even from the class of artistes of the lowest level.

Then, all the specters to which poverty gives a body: hunger cold and fear, came to lay siege to their door and crouch before them. Comparable to a caged bird to which one has forgotten to give its seed, Ferret held himself immobile, closed his eyes and waited. His companion, by contrast, a miracle of affection and devotion, was elevated by courage to heroism. Making a vow to spare him torments and insults, to leave him to his nonchalance and his dreams, she convinced herself that she would have health, life and strength for both of them. The insufficient salary that she drew from labor that obliged her to long wakefulness and exhausted her, soon proved the vanity of her efforts and her hopes.

They lived nevertheless, but in what conditions! What is called Providence is like a miserly father who lacks the courage to forget his child, but who only gives him just enough to ensure that he does not die. A providential hazard threw poor Ferret into the path of an entrepreneur of fairground spectacles who, after hearing him execute a few passages on the violin, judged it appropriate to hire him in order to add to the attraction of his evening amusements. The wretch thus became an adoptive member of a family of Bohemians who had no fixed domicile, who traveled with their house, camping in the open air at the gates of cities, on fairgrounds, and incessantly furrowing the world from the east to the west, the west to the north and the north to the south.

Sustained by his friend, whose presence had at length become pleasant and necessary to him, Ferret rapidly acquired the mores of that new life. He lent himself with an inexhaustible complaisance to the industrial fantasies of his employer, to the point that he soon became in the latter's hands a magnificent source of receipts. His success can be judged by the audacity that the physicist had of eventually selling his booth of planks and canvas in order to put on performances on the stage of veritable theaters.

One day, in Geneva, the walls were suddenly covered with monstrous posters framed with bizarre designs, in which, following a series of more or less seductive promises, the name of Ferret blossomed in gigantic characters.

Those posters, the form, dimension and colors of which could not fail to attract eyes, presented the son of the instrument-maker as a violinist without peer, an extraordinary phenomenon who, while playing the violin "in fifty-seven positions" had excited the admiration and enthusiasm of all the courts of Europe.

At nightfall, the doors were no sooner opened than the floor, the stalls, the boxes, the galleries and the amphitheater were packed with a numerous public enticed by the advertisement of the program. A bad orchestra, the worn-out magic of boxes with double bottoms, the stiffness of automata, the equivocations and clumsiness of a simpleton only served to multiply tenfold the impatience people had to hear the virtuoso. He finally appeared. What a spectacle! To the confusion of the entire hall, they saw a poor old man with a fatigued expression and a trailing step, poorly dressed, who, after having humbly saluted the spectators, delivered himself to all imaginable extravagances. First he held the instrument under the chin, in accordance with the ordinary method; then he placed it between his legs like a cello, and then behind his back; then he lay down, and then had himself tied in a sack; and in all those "positions," which attained the number fifty-seven, he executed a piece of music of contestable charm. The public, struck with amazement, commenced by murmuring, was soon gripped by commiseration. In addition to the fact that they decided not to be irritated by the miscalculation, they even had the generosity to stammer a few ironic bravos, and even to applaud.

In the midst of his perpetual peregrinations, Ferret spent several sojourns in his native land. Once, to the great astonishment of his friend, he was gripped there by a profound, indescribable disturbance. The month of June was about to end; it was a feast-day; admirable weather attracted strollers to the shade of the boulevard where the fair was being held. The perfumes of the atmosphere, the sight of the trees, the sound of ringing church bells, the costumes of the peasants arriving in joyous bands, the colors, the sounds, the odors and the perspectives all acted powerfully on Ferret's soul and awoke therein a vague sentiment of the past.

Furtively, he quit the booth where he worked, cleaved through the growing crowd, reached one of the gates of the city and went in a melancholy fashion along the ditch of the exterior walls. The goal of his excursion was not long in doubt. A road bordered by thorny hedges drew him to the left and led straight to a vast cemetery. For nearly an hour he took pleasure in losing himself in the labyrinth of paths that marked out the cypresses and the tombs. Always turning his gaze from one side to the other with a sustained attention that was not habitual to him, he was preoccupied with deciphering the epitaphs, and seemed to be invaded by an increasing emotion. From turning to turning, his steps bore him toward a remote and forgotten corner, where fragments of stone lay scattered in the freely-growing grass, the inscriptions of which had been effaced by time and rain.

Suddenly, he stopped. A violent sensation made his body tremble. His eyes had just encountered a listing black cross, on the arms of which the slight trace was still legible of the words: *Here lies Antoinette-Françoise Ferret.*

The solitude was profound and the silence was only troubled by vague, distant sounds comparable to the hum of a subterranean city. Upset in the depths of his soul, Ferret seemed to be on the point of suffocating; his legs could no longer sustain him. He fell to his knees, put his hands together, inclined his head and shed torrents of tears.

His companion had followed him at a distance and had soon divined everything.

That pilgrimage was not the only one that he was to make to his mother's grave. On the eve of his departure he returned to it, and noticed, with a mild joy that attracted new tears to his eyes, that the cross had been straightened and stabilized, and that, on the freshly shifted soil, arranged in a mound, a generous hand had planted two magnificent rose-bushes charged with buds and flowers ready to bloom.

The moment was not far off when, worn out, withered and incapable of rousing any sentiment other than that of compassion, he was abandoned by the businessman who was exploiting him. He returned to Paris, never to emerge again, in order to see his breast decorated by a medal there, and to descend there into the ultimate rank of nomadic artistes.

He was no more than a shadow. One might have thought him a body devoid of a soul, an automaton moved by invisible springs. The years, the travels, the melancholy and the self-neglect, had ruined his constitution, taken the gaze from his eyes, hollowed out his cheeks and temples and curbed his back. One could see his silhouette vacillating as he passed by. A decrepit old man, indifferent to everything, he did not hear you if you talked to him, he seemed no longer able to feel heat or cold, or hunger, He went on and on, limping, at random, as the wind blows, under the gaze of his friend, from courtyard to courtyard, café to café, and tavern to tavern, playing fragments of concerts and various tunes for alms, which flowed pell-mell of their own accord beneath his fingers.

However—would you believe it?—in that infimal milieu where he found himself decidedly classified, he encountered one day, without seeking it, the intoxicating glory that he had once pursued in vain for so many years, through the rudest proofs.

By way of preamble, deign to think about the amplitude and flexibility of the word "musician." Between the composer and the cripple who runs his lips over reed flutes, the number of men who have been liberally accorded that title is incalculable. Are not the symphonist of genius, the concert singer, the ungovernable chorist, the village horn-player and the blind fiddler uniformly called musicians? It is necessary to add—a much more curious thing—that there is not one of those artistes, no matter to what category he belongs, who does not have his public to appreciate him, to understand him, admire and recompense him. That is a fact. The public, like the earth on which we tread, is composed of a series of superposed layers, each of which has its degree of intelligence, its sum of knowledge, its tastes, its passions and its arts relative to it.

There would be no point in undertaking to argue that point. The pleasure that one experiences, the emotion one feels, are in art the sovereign reason, and nothing is more respectable than an appreciation based on a sentiment genuinely experienced. Whether a group forms around an accordion player and faints with contentment, takes pleasure in listening to a ridiculous singer of hackneyed ballads, is borne to the clouds by insipid comic operas, or is amused by a banal country dance, while yawning at a strong work full of ideas, it is necessary to agree that all those naïve enthusiasms of ignorance are a thousand times preferable to artificial admirations and conventional infatuations for beautiful things that one does not understand.

A blind man of the bridges was marrying his daughter, and he gave a fête on the occasion of that marriage. It was in the heart of the Saint-Marcel quarter, in a large room decorated with a profusion of benches, chairs and suspended lamps. For a quarter of the guests the palest luminary was, in any case, a futile luxury. All the blind beggars in Paris seemed to have come together there. In the center of that gathering, the elite of a class that, in parentheses, has its language, its mores and its prejudices, the viewpoint was admirable for the study of the extent to which humans, even the humblest, are enemies of equality. One would not have remarked without some surprise that those worthy people had the consolation of seeing below them artistes that they could scorn—for example, those they called disdainfully "organ-grinders" or "peddler-musicians." As for mores, the astonishment would have been no less to hear the Amphitryon say to one of his colleagues: "Talent, no doubt; but that isn't conduct; he isn't married, one can't receive him."

However low Ferret had fallen, he was still, in merit, far superior to the members of that gathering. One could even advance that, for the milieu, he was an artiste just as strange, just as extraordinary as Paganini for the public of the Opéra. At the news that he would honor the soirée with his presence, murmurs of satisfaction rose up from all sides: "Ferret is coming! Ferret is coming!" was repeated in chorus.

"Boy," said a grand old man to his young neighbor, "open your ears well, for tonight you will hear the most famous violinist in Paris."

His arrival caused a sensation; people stood up to do him honor. All of them, great and small, blind and sighted, crowded around him, eager to shake his hand. The worthy man, although he did not understand clearly the motive for that urgency, nevertheless seemed touched by the ovation. His companion conducted him to a chair and sat down beside him. The session commenced.

As in the majority of concert halls, a stage of planks had been set up at the back over which singers, guitarists, harpists, and player of the vielle and the mandolin filed in turn. A duo for harp and violin was followed by a ballad with a cello accompaniment, the sentimental ballad by a comic ditty, that by a flute solo, and so on, according to the order of a program drawn up in advance. During the entr'actes, laden trays circulated, some of pastries and other of various refreshments. By closing one's eyes to the poverty of the decorations, the lack of brightness of the costumes and the lights, one could have believed it a musical soirée of a more elevated society. Between milieux that are supposedly the most dissimilar there are often only differences in form. Most of the time, fundamentally, there are identical customs, analogous fashions of distraction, and the same ways of seeing and feeling; not to mention that these folk, in the fear of singularizing themselves, allowed themselves the indulgence of applauding everything, even mediocrity or nullity, absolutely as is practiced elsewhere.

Before the great ball that was to close the concert and prolong the celebration until morning, Ferret, to whom the program had attributed the role of a bouquet in a firework display, rendered very willingly to the desire that everyone had to hear him. His presence on the stage was saluted by unanimous applause. In spite of the rust of years, and long carelessness, apart from the fact he had never entirely lost the clarity of elocution that he owed to his schooling, he had conserved a certain sentiment of tenderness that could not fail to move the assembly profoundly. In any case, who does not know how much favorable prejudices can lend to the charm and magic of the most insignificant individual? He had not finished the ritornello of a first piece than he was applauded warmly and people cried: "Encore! Encore!"

The poor man raised his eyelids and allowed moist eyes to be seen; a smile wandered over his lips. He continued with a grand Italian aria, streaming with tears. His manner of singing merits mention, and it was all the better because the majority of present masters of song do not profess any other. Every note trembled as if the sonorous waves had been set in vibration by the spring of an electrified watch; his trills were reminiscent of, and might have been mistaken for, the bleating of goats; finally, he slid his fingers over the strings and produced mewlings of an ineffable sweetness. All that, invariably nuanced by the perpetual passage of the most vigorous *forte* of the most nebulous *piano*, and complicated by a veritable efflorescence of flourishes, caused an immense impression.

People clapped their hands as if to break them, and cried again: "Encore! Encore!" That applause and those cries brought the artiste out of his torpor definitively. By the exercises to which he delivered himself thereafter he suddenly provoked an explosion of laughter. One of the guests, in his delight, leaned toward the ear of his neighbor and murmured to him: "Wouldn't you swear that our host has also invited birds to his fête?"

Ferret had, in fact, just imitated with perfect exactitude the songs of various birds, including the call of the cuckoo and that of the quail. He imitated with equal gladness the sounds of the flute, the vielle and the trombone. By dint of success he was gradually enfevered and acquired verve, almost impetuosity. One might have believed momentarily in the resurrection of his faculties. From the depths of his memory, the shreds surged spontaneously of a military symphony supposed to depict all the peripeties of a battle. It was bounding with delight and enthusiasm that the audience recognized successively the sounds of the clarion, the roll of drums, rifle fire, the intermittent thunder of cannon, the whinnying of horses, cavalry charges, the cries of the wounded and dying, and then the victory song of the conqueror and the funeral march of the vanquished.

On the way, he took care not to forget the extravagances that the prestidigitator had taught him. To cite only one example, he concluded with a feat of skill that earned him a triumph without equal. With lightning rapidity, instead of producing the last note of the final flourish with the bow, rotating his violin and parading his moist thumb over the backboard as if over the skin of a Basque drum, without losing the measure, he made the desired note heard quite clearly and accurately. It is necessary to despair of sustaining by expression the violence of transports that buffoonery provoked. For nearly fifteen minutes, the chamber resounded with shrill, frenetic discordant cries, accompanied by a din of clapping hand and stamping feet. One might have thought that one had gone astray in the midst of a troop of furious bacchantes.

That formidable racket penetrated all the way to Ferret's heart and provoked an extraordinary commotion there. His features gradually lost their expression of bewilderment to take on one of attention and anxiety. He inclined an ear, like someone listening. In the depths of his immeasurably magnified orbits, his eyes, with irises comparable to pale and floating lights, appeared to be looking inwards and searching there for memories. One might have thought that he was retracing the course of time, that he was returning to the days of his childhood, that he was remembering his history, recalling his father, his mother, his dreams, his miscalculations, his tortures, and that he was conscious of his madness and his degradation.

At those strange symptoms, his friend had suddenly risen to her feet; frightened and breathless, she observed him with a febrile attention, doubtless dreaming that the soul of the poor man might be disengaged from the thick shell under which the chagrins and the years had buried it.

His shudder, his expression of dolorous surprise, his increasingly moving pantomime—everything, in fact—permitted the conjecture that he had recovered his memory. The muscles of his face relaxed, floods of tears rose from his breast to his eyes; he tried to speak and was prevented by sobs; he inclined his head and extended his arms as if to find a support, and fell full length on the stage.

His companion was already beside him, and enveloped him with tenderness and care, as a mother would have done for her child. The solicitude and urgency of some, the consternation of others and the emotion of all gave the measure of the sympathies that the old man inspired. It was with an indescribable sensation of pleasure that he was seen to reopen his eyes. The anxiety that he had caused was succeeded by a noisy joy, further acclamations, the further stamping of feet and almost savage hurrahs.

If he had really had a few moments of lucidity, at least now he had fallen back into his lethargy. He was weeping even more copiously, but it was with contentment. The admiration, enthusiasm and affection of his colleagues awoke against all expectation a few echoes in his soul, and procured him, incontestably, the greatest happiness that he had ever experienced. And in fact, with regard to what he was today, the relative glory that he collected was worth as much as that of which he had once dreamed in the plenitude of his faculties.

To conclude, with regard to that scene, if one puts it in the context of the life of the poor man, if one recalls that he had sacrificed everything—father, mother, amour, his repose, his life—and that he would have sacrificed a thousand times more, one would have, in that parallel, with a few nuances, the summary history of many others. Only a distracted mind could contradict it.

In our hopes and our dreams, which all too frequently nothing legitimates, there is almost always, between the means one puts to work, the courage, the energy one expends, and the result that one attains, an utterly shocking disproportion. If, impossibly, our hero had realized his dream, should he not have been pitied, in any state of affairs, for purchasing an ephemeral glory at the price of such long fatigues, so many sacrifices and dolors? And to complete his misery, it was necessary— again, a very common detail—that he had not even the capacities of his ambition.

However, miserable as he was, at least he escaped, thanks to the tenderness of an incomparable friend, the abjection of vice. The abnegation and the devotion of that angelic creature, without whom he would infallibly have been even more unhappy, was not belied for a single day. Like the charity of which she was the image, she was unaware of herself, and was as astonished to be praised as to be pitied.

That she was the same person as the young woman once sacrificed by Ferret to vague anxieties it would be difficult to doubt, although, in her invincible modesty, she had constantly eluded any assertion capable of establishing the identity for sure. It seemed that it pleased her to relegate that detail to the shadows, and even to let him believe in two distinct individuals. Nevertheless, both of them could incontestably have borne the name of the saint who, in her surges of amour and her enthusiasm for the Passion, cried: "Either to suffer or to die!"[1]

The secret of her inalterable affection is a less obscure problem. "There is no man so unfortunate or so odious on earth," it is written somewhere, "to whom fate has not attached a companion in his work, in his torture in his crime or in his virtue." The remark is true at all degrees; it is sufficient to open one's eyes or to remember to be certain of it. Where there are consolations to lavish, courage to sustain, sacrifices to make or some act of heroism to accomplish, is one not assured of always encountering a woman?

---

1 This is the usual translation of the motto of Saint Teresa of Avila: *Aut pati aut mori*, although some translators drop the first "to," changing the implication somewhat, and her writings suggest that her actual ambition was to suffer and not to die, in order to continue the glorification of her faith

Major Whittington

NOT far from the gardens of Paris, on the flowery banks of the Seine, a vast and undulating plain extends, where various pleasure houses blossom here and there like great orange dahlias in the midst of vervain. From one of the neighboring hills, the view would be ravishing were it not for a quadrilateral of gigantic walls that dominate the ensemble and obfuscate the scene. Those bare, solid, rusty walls imprison a terrain of about three hectares. The stroller measures the enclosure and runs an eye over them without noticing any other opening than that of a little oak door, which seems to require, in order to open it, the secret of some magical formula, since there is no trace thereon of any lock, handle, knocker or bell. What gives pause and completes the surprise is that, from a distance, by posting oneself at a height and aiding oneself with a telescope, one sees rising up side by side from within, the gilded dart of a lightning-conductor and the thin flue of a factory chimney, from which smoke escapes incessantly in little intermittent jets.

The curious renounce seeing through those walls. Since their erection, no one, to the knowledge of the people in the vicinity, had penetrated into the enclosure and no one had come out. So it was an event when three men arrived, on a foggy afternoon, outside the little door. One of them, distinguished by a red ribbon, marched ahead, and the other two followed with an air of deference. They were evidently representatives of the authority.

This is what had given rise to that domiciliary visit.

Eight or nine days before, a local bourgeois, climbing the steps of the Palais, had been directed to the cabinet of the *procureur général* and had asked to see that magistrate on a matter of the greatest importance. His black coat, his white cravat and his respectable appearance had obtained him the immediate audience that he requested. To begin with, he reeled off his name, forenames, titles of ex-merchant and proprietor, and then continued in a grave voice in harmony with the singularity of his revelations:

"My wife and I, Monsieur le Magistrat, have no other ambition but to live tranquilly in our home; as Horace says: *Felix qui potuit rerum* . . .[1] I have sacrificed the satisfaction of having children to the inconvenience of bringing them up, the fear of hearing their cries and that of raising ingrates. We have not regretted it; it ap-

---

1 Author's note: "In his trouble the excellent man commits blunders"; it is not Horace who said that but Virgil, in book IV of the Georgics." The footnote does not appear in the *Revue française* version of the story, and was presumably added to the book version because a reader of the periodical pointed out the error.

peared wiser to us to divide our wealth into as many lots as months that remain to us hypothetically, to live. In that fashion we enjoy a perfect satisfaction without having to fear falling stock prices, crashes or bankruptcies. While she takes care of the house and supervises our domestics, I smoke, stroll, water our vegetables, occupy myself with the rabbits, trim the trees or pick fruits. Without flattering ourselves, I believe that it would be difficult to find two more virtuous individuals for a hundred leagues around. We have no debts, we never speak ill of our neighbors, we pay our taxes scrupulously, we do not infringe the liberty of anyone; it seems to us that the universe is bounded by the gate of our house."

Here the honorable bourgeois paused. He took a deep breath and continued:

"However, Monsieur le Magistrat, what ought you not to dread from my presence? You have doubtless already sensed it from my facial expression. Have I any need to tell you that our repose has been destroyed, our hopes disappointed, our plans disrupted, and that our happiness is no longer anything but a vanished dream?"

The procureur général, amazed, looked at his visitor with the expression that a physician adopts with a real or supposed hypochondriac. He asked him politely to get to the point.

"Beside our house," the bourgeois went on, "extends a vast terrain enclosed by high walls. The sight of it is somber and mysterious. Those walls, in the beginning, inspired in us the most entire confidence. The owner, jealous enough of his interior to hide it at so much expense, could only be, in our opinion, a tranquil man full of solicitude for the peace of his neighbors. Throughout the winter, in fact, events responded to our expectation. But, God in Heaven, this spring and summer, at this very hour . . ."

"Well?" demanded the magistrate with interest.

"Alas, Monsieur, imagine all the noises of earth and Heaven concentrated to the highest degree within that enclosure. How can I give you an idea of the racket that escapes from it? You would sometimes think it the barking of fifty assembled packs, then the sound of a locomotive pulling a train, then innumerable fanfares, then rifle fire, and then an orchestra of ten thousand musicians, or the din of a tempest with the accompaniment of thunder. In brief, Monsieur, from dusk until dawn, and from dawn until dusk, more often than not, one cannot hear oneself speak for a league around. My wife and I have lost our appetite and sleep, we are plunged into depression and terror, we are disgusted with life; it would not take much for us to die of chagrin and despair."

In the opinion of the magistrate, the grievances of the plaintiff were greatly exaggerated, if they were not entirely imaginary. Unable, at least, to believe that they were seriously founded, he put the supposed maniac off with a vague promise and hastened to get rid of him. In fact, no order was given and no measure taken. A few days later, however, the unfortunate proprietor, beside himself, and with death in his visage, came to renew his depositions and his laments. The decision made by the procureur général could not hold up against the threat of being periodically obsessed; without abandoning his place, he delegated Baron de Sarcus, one of his most intelligent deputies, to verify the extent to which the poor man's strange assertions were exact.

The door opened by itself. Scarcely had the magistrate and the two secretaries that he had brought with him gone in, than the door closed as it had opened, by means of an invisible mechanism.

Everything that they embraced with a glance was strange: the house, the garden, and even the terrain that they had beneath their feet. A domestic came toward them. Their surprise was extreme: that domestic, clad in an ample hazelnut-brown overcoat, as straight and stiff as a pole, was not walking; he was sliding on rails; his eyes, of the finest enamel, lacked expression; it did not seem that blood flowed in his veins, and his lips designed a dry and inflexible line. He stopped. A noise of cogwheels was heard. As he raised his arm to shoulder height like a railway signal, he opened his mouth and articulated the single monosyllable: "There! There!"

At grips with an increasing astonishment, Monsieur de Sarcus headed toward the door that the domestic had indicated. He noticed in passing the curious pedestal on which the house rested: through thick glass as transparent as crystal, his eyes plunged into an inextricable labyrinth of wheels, cylinders, pivots, escapements, anchors, teeth, hooks, pothooks and twenty other pieces of enormous dimension, all entangled and all in motion; it was enough to give one vertigo.

The visitors penetrated then into a vestibule, at the back of which the steps of a staircase began. A multitude of copper buttons dotted the walls. This warning, translated into a familiar idiom, invited prudence:

On pain of death, don't touch anything.

They went up . . .

The stairway ended in a rather poorly illuminated antechamber in which there were several doors. The door facing the staircase had two battens. A domestic in a powdered wig, dressed in the French fashion, in short trousers, silk stockings and buckled shoes, was standing sentinel there; his immobility was that of a tree trunk. Suddenly, he was animated. The two battens of the door, swinging on their hinges, unmasked the view of a vast room inundated by the most beautiful daylight. At the same time, with a stiff and angular gesture, the domestic invited the deputy and his secretaries to enter. They advanced rather timidly to the threshold and plunged anxious gazes into the interior.

"Come in, Messieurs," said a voice.

At first sight, the man who was speaking, a person dressed entirely in red, plunged into an armchair, produced the effect on them of an automaton, but he only had the appearances of one.

"Come in, Messieurs, come in!" he repeated, making a sign with his hand.

They bowed respectfully. The room in which they found themselves, high, wide and profound, admirably illuminated from above, did not contain anything except the red-clad man and his seat. On the other hand, there was no area larger than a handspan on the parquet or along the walls that did not appear to conceal some secret or mystery; the parquet above all, which creaked underfoot, was nothing but an assemblage of trap-doors and marquetry; a thousand intersecting stripes made it resemble a sheet of frozen water on which people had been skating all day. In addition to that, a singular sound, similar to that of the mechanism of a cathedral clock, filled the ears with a perpetual hum. In spite of the noise, one could hear, but as one hears next to the active wheel of a water-mill.

"Sit down, Messieurs," added the unknown man, pressing one of the gilded buttons with which the arms of his chair were studded. Immediately, three comfortable armchairs slowly escaped from the wall.

Although Monsieur de Sarcus did not breathe a word, his eyes spoke for him; they were bursting with questions. His host seemed to have as much difficulty moving as a lizard numbed by cold. His external appearance respired strangeness. Already tall in stature, he was coiffed by a hat with gigantic horns, which made him seem even taller. That hat, buried under a flood of black plumes, crowned a face that was noble and intelligent, but dogmatic and impassive. White hair garnished the temples; the forehead was broad and undulating; between two eagle eyes, which shone in the shadow of thick gray eyebrows, an enormous nose was rooted, thin and curved, comparable to that of the Italian Polchinelle. A bitter disdain creased his lips; the strong square chin announced a powerful will; on the edge of his side-whiskers, no less white than his hair and trimmed at the level of the mouth, excessively small pink ears expanded.

The red coat in which the individual was dressed attracted the eyes at first; it was only later that one saw his black culottes, the buckles of which were lost in the legs of a pair of boots with golden tassels.

"I was expecting you, Monsieur le Baron," he said, phlegmatically.

By his accent, a foreigner was divinable. Monsieur de Sarcus was not mistaken about that.

"You know me, Milord?" he exclaimed.

"Are you not Monsieur de Sarcus," replied the man, still calmly, "distinguished scientist and eminent magistrate? Are these messieurs not your secretaries? Is not the younger one your nephew, Philippe de Sarcus, a young advocate of whom much is hoped?"

"I have no need to inform your lordship, then," observed the intrigued deputy, "of the object of my mission?"

"And it will be a veritable pleasure for me, Monsieur, to aid you in the investigation confided to you."

One could not be more courteous.

"But you've had a long journey, Messieurs," added the Englishman. "Before we begin, allow me to offer you some refreshment."

Before the thought had even occurred to the visitors to refuse, he touched a pedal fitted into the parquet with his foot. A door opened; through that doorway a third domestic penetrated into the room, rolling, and stopped two paces away from his master.

"John," said the latter, "serve Madeira for these Messieurs and me."

The domestic made a gesture of intelligence, pirouetted on his heels, and left as he had entered. He reappeared after a very brief interval; his right hand supported a tray on which four full glasses and biscuits were arranged, which he presented first to the deputy, then to the secretaries, and then to his master. They drank, but not before having bowed to one another politely.

After that, John, retracing his steps, and describing the same circuit, collected the empty glasses and disappeared. The door closed again.

A long silence fell.

"You see me, Milord," said the baron, suddenly, "confounded by astonishment. I can scarcely believe my senses; it seems that I am dreaming."

"Pooh!" said the lord disdainfully. "In these childish matters, Vaucanson was my master. Wait, Monsieur . . ."[1]

At the same time as he had activated the pedal in the parquet, he had pressed the arm of his chair with his fingers; a carillon responded to it. Time went by; it was almost that of an alarm clock.

"It will only be a moment, Monsieur," said the Englishman. "You seem to be anxious to know how, without quitting my armchair, without receiving any

1 The inventor Jacques Vaucanson (1709-1782) built numerous automata, regarded at the time as trivial amusements, but which left a long impression in the memory and achieved a remarkable legendary celebrity that gave rise to numerous literary works in the fledgling genre of *roman scientifique* before and after the present example.

paper or person, I am able to receive news, I had fore-seen that anxiety. The carillon you have just heard will furnish me with the opportunity to respond to you."

With a scarcely perceptible pressure, he caused a small table to emerge from the floor to his right, at the center of which was a dial, and he continued: "At this moment, Monsieur, something new is happening in China."

The needle of the dial began to move and the caril-lon recommenced.

"The Emperor of the Celestial Empire," said the Englishman, his eyes fixed on the dial, "is decreeing gifts to industrialists who are coming to establish them-selves in his country. He is sending a commission of mandarins, in steam junks, to visit the establishments of Europe."

At that point, the needle stopped, which put an end to the carillon.

"That's fabulous!" exclaimed the baron, enthusiasti-cally.

A carillon of a different timbre announced that the needle was about to speak again.

"Philadelphia," said the major. "The *Saturn*, a mon-ster locomotive constructed in accordance with my system. Frightful accident. Pleasure train, carrying fifty thousand people. Ten thousand killed. One shudders at the thought of what might happen, etc. . . ."

The vibrations of a third bell came in time to inter-rupt the consternation of the deputy and his secretaries.

"Aha!" said the Englishman, slightly emotional this time. "New Holland is in full revolution. The populations are rising from one end of the country to the other. Merchants are meeting in Melbourne to proclaim the independence of the Australian states. Separation from the motherland has been decreed. It's a question of constituting a realm. A convict has been chosen as king."

At the immobility of the needle, the Englishman, after a few minutes, declared that for the moment, there was no longer anything new or interesting under the sky.

However, a fourth carillon suddenly rang out.

"This time, Messieurs," said the Englishman, "the warning concerns you. The procureur général is anxious about the danger you might be running and is thinking of sending you help."

"Inform him, Milord, if it is possible," said the deputy, swiftly, "that we are safe and, better than that, in the company of the most amiable of men."

As soon as the lord had satisfied that request, he said: "Presently, Monsieur, you can see how easy it is for me to reach an understanding with suppliers. To hide nothing from you, the objects that I might need are not numerous; my chemistry and my industry substitute for almost everything. To cite only one example, the wine you have drunk and the biscuits you have eaten are of my composition."

"Is that possible?" said Monsieur de Sarcus. "My word! I give you my compliments, Milord, the wine and the biscuits were delicious."

"That's nothing, less than nothing," said the Englishman, modestly. "What merchant would not remonstrate with me on that chapter? I will confide to you summarily that the four walls of this property embrace an entire petty universe, of which I can call myself the creator. My science, my sagacity and my imagination have rendered me the rival, almost the equal, of nature; it would not take much for me to surpass her. Except for the art of creating living beings, which is, to say the least, unnecessary and vain, I do not know that I can be asked to execute anything impossible. You can judge for yourselves."

"I believe you, Milord," replied Monsieur de Sarcus, immediately, "I believe you. Only one detail confounds me: how is it that a man of your value is unknown?"

"Do you not know Major Whittington?" said the red-clad man, in the simplest and most modest tone.

At that name, the features of the deputy betrayed a profound emotion; he seemed momentarily thunderstruck. Enthusiasm rapidly snatched him out of that stupor.

"Have I heard correctly?" he exclaimed, rising to his feet—and his example was followed by his two secretaries. "I have before my eyes the savant, illustrious and immortal Major Whittington, the incomparable astronomer, the fabulous mechanician, the inventor, the creator of the new panification, of the infallible macrobiotic, of the new telescope, thanks to which the planets no longer have any mystery for us, and a thousand other marvels—the man, in sum, whom the century has proclaimed with a unanimous voice to be a Pico della Mirandola to the fourteenth power?"

With an inclination of the head, the major said yes to everything.

"Oh, Milord," said Monsieur de Sarcus, at the paroxysm of his enthusiasm, "this day fulfills my ambition, since I owe to it the honor of knowing the most marvelous genius that has illustrated or will ever illustrate humankind!"

Major Whittington was impassive before these eulogies; none of the muscles of his face stirred; his icy phlegm was inalterable. To his admirer, who was astonished to see such a great individual cloistered in an obscure retreat, hiding from glory, crowns, honors, the throne and the worship that the universality of his contemporaries were yearning to award him, he replied: "A succinct account of my misfortunes will explain the legitimacy of my misanthropy; a few words will suffice . . ."

In those days, thanks to steam, gas, machines and innumerable human inventions, the level of dolor had considerably diminished on earth. What had once been only a simple prick with a lancet became, in view of that diminution, a large and cruel wound; the slightest contradiction produced on a human being effects as disastrous as what were once called woes and catastrophes. Under the empire of that state of things, Major Whittington had suffered horribly; his life offered nothing but an uninterrupted sequence of disasters. He had scarcely emerged from adolescence than his parents left him master of a considerable fortune and thus deprived him of being the child of his endeavors. Shortly afterwards, an aged bachelor uncle he had never seen had died of an indigestion of joys and bequeathed him, with a prodigious fortune, titles that constituted him one of the most important individuals in the realm.

With less energy he would have died of despair or committed suicide; his great virtue triumphed over cowardly discouragement. Scornful of prejudices, disdaining the duties of his estate, he confined himself in solitude and plunged into the study of the sciences, which had always been his passion: chemistry, physics, mechanics, astronomy, medicine, physiology, philosophy and metaphysics, he devoured everything and showed himself superior to everything. His late nights, his labors, his schemes, his industry and his imagination had enriched the arts and sciences with a series of discoveries and masterpieces each more astonishing than the last. Why? In order to see himself misunderstood, shamed, calumniated, pillaged and persecuted by the very people he enriched.

Judge by one example. He invented the famous telescope that bears his name; it is a known marvel. With that telescope, which only cost a million, one can stroll on the moon as in the gardens of the neighborhood. What a service! Well, it was claimed that he had bought that discovery at a price of gold from a poor and forgotten industrialist.

That was not all. Nearly two centuries before, a prize had been offered to the scientist who succeeded in reforming the tide tables.[1] For him, it was child's play; his calculations were infallible. The elements conspired

---

1 If this refers to the prize offered by the French Académie des Science in 1738 for a theory of tides, it would suggest that the story is set in the early twentieth century.

against him. Because brutal facts dared to belie him, because the sea had the impertinence to contradict his imperishable reforms by twenty minutes, the prize was refused to him. That revolting iniquity brought his misfortunes to a culmination. Resolved to end an existence forever withered and poisoned, he realized his fabulous fortune and bought a commission in the Indian Army.

"I had decided," the major said, at this point, "to allow myself to die, of the climate or war. Death refused me; there was no war, and the climate was full of respect for me. I thought that one could not be more miserable. I was wrong. My excessive riches were an irresistible magnet, which, at length had gathered around me all the adventuresses and dowryless misses in Great Britain; I was the focal point of the most beautiful and most dangerous eyes in the world.

"A blonde and rosy creature, truly angelic in appearance, succeeded in turning my head; I fell madly in love. Our marriage was celebrated with an extraordinary pomp. We had palaces, gardens on the banks of the Godavari, thousands of servants and elephants; we led a princely existence. I believed that I was understood, and the wounds on my heart were beginning to scar over when, at the hour when I least expected it, I surprised the person that I had made the equal of a queen . . . absorbed in the elucubration of stanzas to the stars. *I had married a bluestocking!* A thunderbolt would have caused me less surprise; I could have fallen from the tenth floor, head first, and the impact would have been less rude.

"Under the empire of the fury that possessed me, flames devoured the stanzas, and the caimans of the Godavari the perfidious creature. After that, I tried to die. The thrust deviated; I gave myself a wound that had no other consequence than that of changing the direction of my ideas. Impatient at having been until then the most unfortunate of mortals, the fantasy took me to become the most fortunate, and to direct all my future efforts to that goal.

"My certainty, drawn from the springs of incessant speculations, was that the key to perfect happiness resides in the art of surpassing others. I quit India, I abjured my ingrate homeland and I came incognito to establish myself in this plain. Experience has proved me right; I have succeeded beyond my expectations; if I still suffer, it is from monotony, and I am sometimes reduced by it to causing myself some harm in order to be less happy."

Monsieur de Sarcus, deeply distressed, admitted that it would be necessary to go back at least a century to find misfortunes as poignant as those that had just struck his ears; he congratulated the major on the serenity that he had finally achieved.

"Although." he added, "I can only take account very imperfectly of the manner in which Milord, in a sequestration so absolute, can employ his time."

"Know, Monsieur," replied Lord Whittington, "that six weeks, at the most, would suffice for an examination of the distractions that I can procure without leaving home. It will please you, I hope, to see the principal ones. Let us proceed methodically. A man of your merit ought to like traveling, with all the more passion because his duties scarcely suffer that he can satisfy his penchant. Toward what country would Monsieur de Sarcus fly if, impossibly, he were suddenly impelled by wings?"

Meanwhile night had fallen gradually in the room; a profound darkness soon reigned there.

"Toward Peking, Saint Petersburg, Philadelphia or even Japan?" continued the major. "Deign to tell me."

The love of travel had, indeed, always possessed Monsieur de Sarcus. He confessed, at hazard, the desire that had pursued him for a long time to see India. Immediately, a sort of creaking was heard, and the immense wood paneling at the back of the room disappeared gradually, to allow the sight, under the radiance of a bright sun, of perspectives of an incomparable splendor. The pagodas, the edifices, the gardens, the countryside and a thousand other details of the perspectives had the dimensions, the relief, the brightness and the animation of nature itself; it was magical, intoxicating and sublime.

Monsieur de Sarcus was able to compensate his passion in abeyance. Before his dazzled eyes filed, by turns, Calcutta, Benares, Delhi, Jaggernath and the most interesting viewpoints of Bengal and the kingdom of Mysore. His enthusiasm no longer had any limits; he was almost mad with joy. By means of an incomprehensible prodigy, the entire world had fallen, in a fashion, into his hand. He expressed the desire to go to China, to the Cape, to the heart of the two Americas, to Tierra del Fuego, and he was immediately transported there.

For the first time, the major quit his armchair. Because of his enormously long legs, he was even taller standing up that he had been judged to be when sitting down; his appearance really had something imposing.

"Now, Messieurs," he said, with his most automatic phlegm, "if it is agreeable to you, we shall go down into the garden . . ."

He had already obtained such an empire over his guests that, penetrated by an almost religious enthusiasm, they stood up without saying a word and followed him.

At the bottom of the staircase, the major said to them: "Would these Messieurs not be charmed to make a tour of my park? I have a locomotive at my discretion. While awaiting dinner we can chat as easily in a carriage, in the open air, as up there . . ."

Before Baron de Sarcus and his secretaries had recovered from the amazement that these offers caused them, a locomotive, docile to the orders of a mechanic, escaped from one of the lateral faces of the house; it was towing an elegant uncovered carriage, in which the major invited his guests to take places.

Immediately, the machine, with a mobile impetus, veered to the right without there being any need for a turntable, vomited smoke, blew out steam, whistled and set forth. Its speed was regulated to that of a pleasure train. The passengers were able to enjoy at their ease the views of the sites through which they passed. It was a varied and very curious spectacle: from the luxury, the brightness and the variety of the flowers, plants and trees that grew and flourished here and there, it was easy to experience an illusion and to believe oneself in the climate richest in plants and precious shrubs; exquisite odors embalmed the atmosphere; groves of orange trees, lemon trees and pomegranates, all laden with fruit, spread shade there in profusion.

On emerging from the woods, the eyes were struck by plantations of sugar cane, rice-fields, a nursery of coffee, cotton and tea bushes. Further on, they traversed a forest of banana trees, coconut palms and breadfruit trees, not to mention the fountains where all sorts of aquatic birds were playing under the intersecting fire of water jets, flowering bushes where warblers, finches and nightingales sang by turns, meadows in which a herd of gazelles reposed, and thickets where wild beasts were lying low.

Through all these riches the train described curves of an incredible boldness, turning to the right and the left, making a hundred tours and detours, without ever traversing the same landscapes, so well that after an hour, at a moderate speed, the major's guests did not believe that they had measured the full extent of the park.

Meanwhile, Lord Whittington, leaning on the cushions, his eyes full of fog, with a dreamy expression, spoke about this, that and the other.

"Our ancestors," he said, "were afraid of everything; their eyes were closed to the simplest ideas. Thus, war and pestilence doubtless frightened them, and yet they were even more fearful of the radical annihilation of those scourges. They seemed to be convinced that such an annihilation would lead to a deplorable and deadly increase in population and would end up making the world too small. What an aberration! How did it escape them that, if room were lacking in breadth and width, we would naturally obtain it in height and build in the sky?"

"As witness, Milord," Monsieur de Sarcus hastened to add, "the plan submitted at this moment to the General Council of the Seine, which the council will not fail to adopt enthusiastically . . ."

"To superpose on Paris," the major continued, tranquilly, "by mean of open frameworks and glass floors, a city no less large and no less beautiful than that capital."

"You know that plan?"

"It's mine: one of my old ideas. The surrounding towns and villages will be razed and all that land delivered to agriculture, successively cleared, plowed, and sown and harvested with machines moving at twenty leagues an hour."

"Oh, with Your Lordship," said the baron, "steps to the sublime are required!"

"There is also the direction of aerostats," the major continued. "Perhaps human intelligence has never shown itself more ingenious than in the examination of that problem, so I can't be sufficiently astonished that such a simple thing has escaped the sagacity of seekers for more than a century.[1] Of what is it a question, in fact? Of tricking the wind, given that one cannot

---

1 Given that the question of directing aerostats first became a topic of enthusiastic discussion in the 1790s, this remark again suggests that the story is set in the early twentieth century.

subjugate it. The air, in its variations and its caprices, must be subject to invariable laws. My observations have taught me those laws; I've drawn up a chart; it informs one, with infinite detail, for all latitudes and for all atmospheric layers, of the direction and degree of the strength of the wind from day to day, hour to hour and second to second; tempests, gusts of wind and whirlwinds are foreseen there. In sum, with the aerostat of my friend Ottway and my chart of air currents, one can go by balloon, in any weather, from one point to another without running any risk."

The locomotive was still traveling.

"Now I think of it, Milord," said Monsieur de Sarcus swiftly, "are not the aerial sanitaria about which Doctor Pritchard is making so much noise, also yours?"

"That's very little, in fact," replied the major. "A child could have thought of that. You know that Pritchard cures all maladies with the aid of atmospheric baths. A very small obstacle hinders the general employment of his system: the difficulty of procuring instantly, in sufficient quantity, the quality of air required by the condition of the invalid. Pritchard was one of my friends; I communicated a plan to him; He is in the process of realizing it. Pretty cottages, drowned in flowers and shrubs, will be raised up by immense aerostats and maintained by cables that will permit them to be fixed in one region of the atmosphere or another. The doctor, equipped with an eudiometer, will make the ascension with his patients, install them, confide them to the care of an intern, and descend again to his home by means of a parachute."

Monsieur de Sarcus, wonderstruck, seemed to doubt that the major could furnish new elements to his admiration.

"Well, Monsieur," said the major, extending his hand, "cast your eyes around you. Everything that strikes your senses, these superb flowers, these rare trees, these golden fruits, these singing birds, these grazing quadrupeds, all these things are due to my artistry. There is not a grain of dust between these four walls that is not my creation. I wish I had the time to show you all the peripeties of a hunt; under these sheds a baying pack of hounds reposes, beaters who sound fanfares, grooms, and a magnificent horse, the gentlest in the world to ride. Or I could animate the fish that are asleep in the depths of those pools, and enable you to angle for eels, pike, trout or salmon. You could also feel all the emotions of a voyage through the stormiest seas, in the elegant gondola suspended over there between the branches of that cedar. But it's getting late . . ."

"In truth, Milord," said the confused baron, "I would scarcely dare to recount what I have seen; no one would be found to add faith to the things that are happening here; the story would be accused of being fabulous and extravagant, the issue of a delirious mind."

The carriage stopped.

"Let's get down, Messieurs," said the major. "I flatter myself that I've given you an appetite."

They went back into the house and went up to the first floor again.

A splendidly served table awaited them. Twenty enormous chandeliers wrought and sculpted in gold hung down from the ceiling, from the branches of which hung festoons and clusters of precious stones; under the floods of light that spread from the only one of those chandeliers that was illuminated, over the finest and whitest tablecloth, where four place-settings were arranged, wines, liqueurs, meats, terrines, etc. were distributed, along with sparkling flowers, silverware and crystal. Nothing was more magnificent or more rejoicing to see.

Each of the guests sat down at the place assigned to him. The table abounded in delicate and tasty dishes; everything was judged exquisite and succulent; every bite and every mouthful was accompanied by a murmur or expression of satisfaction. The magistrate and his secretaries began to be subject to the influence of the spirituous liquors; a kind of exaltation invaded them; they drank, ate, chatted and seemed henceforth to be beyond the state of being astonished, even by the resurrection of the dead.

Lord Whittington encouraged them.

"Eat, Messieurs," he said, "drink! You have nothing to fear in my home from poisons. All these aliments, all these wines, these cold meats, these marinades, conserves, spices and liqueurs emerge from my laboratory."

They reached the dessert. Heady wines flowed in abundance; they drank toasts to chemistry, to mechanics, to the major, and to nature. A slightly noisy gaiety gradually succeeded the serenity of the beginning. Even the cold Whittington took part in it; his tongue loosened, and the grave evidence of a surprising loquacity.

His eloquence, overexcited by numerous draughts of liquor, attained vertiginous heights. The moment was propitious. His repugnance for metaphysical speculations was beyond measure; he had only devoted himself by virtue of ambition to resolving definitively the problem that metaphysicians delighted in resolving anew every fifty years. A volume in press, that would appear in due course, would impose silence forever on inventors of turbulence. He deigned, provisionally, to do no less than deliver his verdict on creation, on the origin, destiny and ends of the human species, and in terms so neat and limpid that the people least versed in those matters would have understood. In the opinion of the baron, it would be necessary to be devoted to an incurable intellectual blindness to refuse to believe, and to contradict.

Nevertheless, the latter, at the paroxysm of his enthusiasm, esteemed that Milord would be no less happy to see, from time to time, elite individuals, notably the faces of women.

"Oh," said the major, "I don't lack society. You'll see Milady, Miss Whittington, Miss Jeanne, Mistress Ingram . . ."

A clock chimed.

"Seven thirty-five and four seconds," added the major. "In the meantime, Messieurs, unless music irritates you, I shall have the honor of enabling you to hear the serenade of a great orchestra."

"What! His Lordship also has an orchestra at his orders?"

"Better than that, Monsieur: a creative orchestra, which improvises what it executes, and the ever-new combinations of which strangely eclipse the taste for the best symphonies of the past. The source of my enjoyments is inexhaustible. Fatigued by harmony, I have recourse to painting or plasticity; Apelles and Phidias would not disown the series of dazzling paintings and admirable sculptures that I obtain by means of the mechanisms of my invention. Time is lacking my desire to show you my resources; I shall limit myself to putting before your eyes, shortly, small-scale models of my most ingenious discoveries."

His Lordship had not finished speaking when the orchestra was already playing a prelude. It was still permissible to converse; a dozen instruments at the most were executing quietly an introduction of the most majestic slowness. The progressive selling of the sounds soon drowned out the major's voice; all instruments known and unknown vibrating successively and collectively aided the scherzo, which suddenly sounded and amused the ear with pirouettes and buffooneries. It would not have taken much for the volume of the racket to exceed the auditory sense, and yet, nothing of the sort happened.

A hymn inspired by the national anthem, "God Save the King," suddenly burst forth violently; the number of instruments, gradually tripled, quintupled and multiplied tenfold, was borne to more than a hundredfold as it approached closer to the terminus of development; in the last part of the finale, notably, the din achieved the furthest limits of the possible. Imagine for a moment the heat of a battle, when drums, clarions, rifles, canons, shells, mortars, the screams of the dying and the hurrahs of soldiers are resonating in chorus—and more! Perhaps, in order to complete the comparison, it would have done no harm to combine it with the rumble of thunder in the mountains. Oh, the shade of that monstrous composer, who dreamed of monstrous orchestras and monstrous concerts, and realized monstrous effects, which, of course, never made only the windows tremble . . . the shade, we say, of that great man, that precursor, would have been content![1]

However, Monsieur de Sarcus was drowsy; he fell asleep for about a quarter of an hour. Under the empire of digestion and the harmonic masses of the orchestra, slumber had gained him. Silence woke him up again; he opened his eyelids slightly, only to lower them immediately; the intensity of the light that inundated his eyes obfuscated them. Blinking furiously, he adapted to the blaze with which the hall was resplendent.

An unexpected, curious, dazzling spectacle struck his eyes; he imagined for a few moments that he was caught by the enchantment of a dream, or the hallucinations of a fever; the twenty chandeliers were ablaze; enormous mirrors, magnificently framed, covered three sides of the hall; between those mirrors, golden arms protruded from the walls, the fingers of which gripped candelabra with numerous candlesticks, similarly lit. A gigantic battle freshly painted, strewn with a multitude

---

1 The intended reference is surely to Hector Berlioz (1803-1869), whose perennial interest in technology and the music of the future led him to produce the utopian fantasy *Euphonia* (1844).

of bloody scenes, with distant horizons where army corps were maneuvering, covered the fourth expanse of wall, which measured a full sixty feet in width and forty in height. To the right, rich armchairs, arranged as in the theater, filled half the floor, empty a little while before. The center was occupied by an immense table, the cloth of which disappeared under small boxes incrusted with gold and tortoiseshell, veritable jewels destined for usages that their form did not indicate. To the left, at intervals, were a sideboard laden with golden vessels, an upright rosewood piano, an elegant occasional table on which a tea service was sparkling, and various gaming tables.

Three superbly dressed women and a young cavalier costumed as a naval officer were playing cards silently at one of the tables; a fourth woman, occupied in embroidery, completed the group. Further away, the major was sitting opposite a bald old man, with whom he was playing a game of chess. At two other tables, Monsieur de Sarcus distinctly saw one of his two secretaries tranquilly playing tric-trac and the other dominoes, each with a stranger. It is necessary to add that Monsieur de Sarcus could only see the backs of his nephew's adversary, that of his other secretary and that of the major.

Somewhat confused by his forgetfulness, the baron got up in haste and leaned over the group of women. On examining the group attentively, he thought once again that he was the victim of a dream, and raised his hand to his eyes. The oldest was an ardent blonde; she had a ruddy complexion; her porcelain blue eyes gazed without seeing; her smile, seemed to be stereotyped upon the violet lips; diamonds and rubies shone amid the gold of her hair; a magnificent pearl necklace embraced her long neck; floods of lace garnished her bodice and the three flaps of her dress. She was playing whist with two young women, one blonde and pink, the other brunette and pale, and a young officer.

Those five persons, including the other woman whose fingers were occupied in embroidery, had erect heads, inanimate faces, stiff bodies; the usage of speech seemed unknown to them; they only moved their forearms and hands, and those only jerkily. All of it was strange and produced the effect of a nightmare.

The peripeties of the game absorbed completely the major and the baron's two secretaries. Monsieur de Sarcus had plenty of time to examine their adversaries. Between them and the group sitting at the whist table, the identity was not in doubt; they were equally mute and equally impassive; their gazes and their features had the same rigidity; the forearms and hands were the only parts of their bodies that moved.

"Checkmate!" a hoarse voice suddenly exclaimed, amid a sound of cogwheels. It was that of the major's adversary.

The latter confessed that he was beaten; he raised his eyes, and only then perceived his guest.

"Pardon me, Monsieur," he said politely. "At grips with the emotions of the game, I forgot about you. Let me introduce you to my family."

He led the stupefied magistrate to the whist table. Scarcely had he touched the group than the three women and the young officer interrupted the game and bounded to their feet as if lifted up by springs. The woman who was embroidering nearby stopped her needle and stood up with the same vivacity.

"I introduce to you Milady," said Lord Whittington, indicating the woman with golden hair.

Monsieur Sarcus bowed. A singular noise was heard; Milady nodded her head, opened her mouth and stammered: "Milord handsome, Milord good, me like Milord."

With that, Milady nodded her head again, bowed, and glided toward the tea table.

"Miss Whittington," continued the major, his hand caressing the cheek of the blonde and rosy young woman.

In her turn, the latter nodded her head, parted her lips and articulated quite clearly: "Papa, Papa." Then she went to join her mother.

With less ceremony, the major introduced successively Henry Smith, a young naval officer engaged to Miss Whittington; Miss Anna, the young and pale brunette, the latter's governess; and Mistress Ingram, lady companion, the embroiderer. Like Milady and Miss Whittington, the three individuals bowed and then headed—with the exception of Smith, who sat down again—in the direction of the table where Milady was already pouring the contents of a fuming teapot adroitly into little china cups.

Then the major drew his guest toward the other gaming tables. He neglected to introduce the unknown persons, but limited himself to naming them.

"The bald gentleman," he said, "is the venerable Sir Norton, the most skillful chess player who has ever existed; he has just beaten me again; I must always resign myself to that. Your nephew is presently playing tric-trac with Sir George Chalmers, rear admiral, and Milady's father. As for your secretary, he's playing dominoes with Sir Barclay, esquire, former consul and one of my oldest friends. Let's not disturb them; they'll be finished soon."

Monsieur de Sarcus examined the players with a feverish curiosity.

"Lost! Lost!" repeated the baron's secretaries, almost simultaneously.

They stood up; their faces expressed chagrin, but not astonishment. Monsieur de Sarcus went to interrogate them. At the same moment, Miss Whittington, Miss Anna and Mistress Ingram offered the messieurs tea and sandwiches, with an exemplary good grace.

"Mistress Ingram," added the major, addressing his guests, "not only embroiders to perfection, she also plays the piano admirably. I hope she won't refuse to let us hear something."

The major took Mistress Ingram's hand and led her to the piano, where she sat down. There was no preamble, Mistress Ingram immediately improvised an original theme that she followed with five or six variations; the first was in triolets, the second in arpeggios, the third in tremolo, that last in cascades and runs. Her finger struck the keys stiffly, the ivory resonated as if under little hammers. One could not say that her playing was very expressive, but at least it had a perfect regularity and equality.

Then Miss Anna was asked to sing. She opened an enormous mouth, which disfigured her, and made vocalizations heard. Her sonorous contralto voice, striking and metallic, embraced four full octaves; that unique voice went from the lowest notes to the highest with a marvelous facility. She executed the liveliest trills, the most rapid runs and the most surprising perilous leaps, without fear and without fatigue. Nothing more perfect could be heard. The little audience was delighted; Milady, especially, approved with head, hands and tongue; at every phrase she repeated; "Brava! Brava! Brava!"

Miss Anna finally rolled back to her place. The orchestra was heard again. On perceiving Henry Smith seize Miss Whittington's waist and match her pace, Monsieur de Sarcus understood that the young couple were going to waltz. In fact, after a few slow measures and a pause, the orchestra burst forth in joyful tones and the two fiancés, holding one another at arm's length, spun in measure, rather like the wooden waltzers of Tyrolean toys. They did not remain in place but described a circuit around the tables and accelerated the movement at the whim of the incessantly more rapid rhythm of the orchestra. That rapidity increased constantly, the forms of the two fiancés becoming less and less distinct; finally, nothing was visible but a single form of indecisive color, the spinning of which resembled a veritable whirlwind. A sign from the major stopped them dead. They returned to their places without appearing to be either emotional or out of breath.

Monsieur de Sarcus did not yet have the assurance of being fully awake; his doubt in that regard caused him a kind of torture. Inclined to believe that he was the victim of a hallucination, however, he was astonished by a perception so clear and persistent of the same milieu, the same people and the same things. Could he admit that a dream might last such a long time, and be connected with so much logic, without any kind of dissolution of continuity?

He was feeling a sort of dolorous oppression, which he attributed to those reflections, when the major said to him: "Presently, Monsieur de Sarcus, while Milady resumes and finishes her game of whist, and while awaiting the ballet-pantomime that I count on having performed for you, we can, if you wish, make a tour of this table and pass in review the ensemble of my finest discoveries."

They went along the long table encumbered by veneered and varnished boxes. Those boxes differed from one another in form and dimension; some were no more voluminous than a snuff-box, whereas others had the caliber on a traveling-bag. Monsieur de Sarcus' memory, although excellent, was insufficient for the number of small-scale models that the major set before his eyes. Each box contained a microscopic machine. Included in the collection were a machine to tailor clothing, an embroidery machine, machines for manufacturing beer, tea and coffee, a machine for trimming beards, others for producing vegetables and fruits, wrapping chocolate, laying eggs, curling hair, washing linen, forging iron, etc., etc. The major did not neglect to put in relief the inappreciable benefits of all these discoveries. With the complete assemblage of agricultural machinery, a single peasant was sufficient to farm ten hectares and more; with another, only one worker would be needed for the exploitation of the largest factory. At least two thirds of men would no longer have anything else to do but fold their arms. Tasks that had once required the hand of a skillful worker could now be obtained with the aid of a mechanism.

The majority of those marvels only obtained a rapid glance from Baron de Sarcus; he was scarcely interested in any machines except those that tended to suppress intelligence; the machine for drawing and painting, for example, the machine for sculpting, the machines for composing music, versifying, carrying out the most complex mathematical operations and, above all, the sketch of a machine for calculating the probabilities of anything, struck him with admiration.

"Truly, Milord," he cried, "one can say that human genius cannot go any further, and that after you, it will be necessary to close the era of inventors and inventions."

He did not turn his head, however, at the very end of the field; certain noises troubled him; the two battens of the door to the drawing room never ceased opening to give passage, sometimes to a military man decorated with medals, sometimes to a gentleman in a black suit, sometimes to a woman clad in velvet, covered in flowers and jewels. Those individuals, in the most various guises, could not hide their family resemblance. Announced successively by the barking of the domestic standing at the entrance, they filed, smiling, as far as Milady, inclined before her and went in an orderly manner to take possession of seats facing the painted wall.

The baron forgot momentarily to take account of those details. He suddenly perceived that the seven or eight long rows of armchairs were filled by a numerous and brilliant company. Whispers comparable to the sound of twenty thousand watches in the same room filled his ears.

His amazement was boundless. On seeing all those stiff and motionless people sitting like rows of onions, folded at right angles, he thought for a moment that he had gone astray in the middle of an assembly of Egyptian gods.

Gradually, the music covered the sound of conversations. The major had already warned his friends, obligingly, that the ballet was about to start, and asked them to take their places.

A ballet! thought Monsieur de Sarcus, confused. *Where? How?*

He attached himself once again to the idea that he was dreaming, that all the things that filed before him participated in slumber or the phantasmagoria of fever.

Once again, he did not have the leisure to verify that hypothesis. Under the influence of the nebulous motifs of the orchestra, he plunged rapidly, involuntarily, into the realm of enchantment.

The immense painting that covered the side of the room toward which the spectators were turned shuddered unexpectedly, like the surface of a pond under the evening breeze. What had at first had the solidity of a wall was no longer anything but painted canvas. About two-thirds of that canvas, gradually raised, unmasked a wide and profound theater, and, to the sounds of a music doubtless appropriate to the pantomime of characters, the performance commenced.

A guide would not have been superfluous; the most intrepid decipherer of hieroglyphs would have recoiled before the task of penetrating the action; no more obscure scenario had ever served as a pretext for dancing. It was evidently a matter of a prince and princess whose union, inscribed in the book of destinies, suffered ten or twelve tableaux of delay. The powers of the fantastic world, interested, some in the mortification and others in the glory of an invincible amour, struggled mightily with ruses, prodigies and acts of courage.

Furthermore, nothing could be imagined more beautiful than the stage setting; it was enough to make the sun itself pale. The sets changed every scene, and the changes of view were operated with lightning rapidity; there was scarcely time to see them; it seemed that one was at the window of a carriage traveling through beautiful landscapes.

A castle besieged by giants and defended by dwarfs was succeeded by a legion of fays fighting hand to hand with genii; an oscillation of hideous witches around a cauldron gave way to quadrilles of butterflies in the middle of a garden where the flowers were animate and joined in with the dances; there were also caverns full of reptiles and monsters, perilous forests populated by phantoms, bats and a thousand chimeras.

All those characters crossed paths, dancing in a fashion to make one faint with ease. Turning their heads to the right and the left, rolling their eyes, they moved their arms like fantoccini, while, sometimes sliding on one leg, sometimes on the other, they seemed held to the floor like iron to a magnet. A pond charged with semi-frozen skaters would not have caused a more singular sensation. Magnificent costumes distinguished the subjects; the principal dancer, for instance, was covered with precious stones. It was necessary to place her in the number of the greatest artistes. She executed various steps and pirouetted on tiptoe with a lighting rapidity that excited the transports of the public periodically.

The curtain finally fell on the inevitable triumph of the two lovers in an atmosphere resplendent with fireworks. Monsieur de Sarcus had understood absolutely nothing; nevertheless, incessantly solicited by a music that was dramatic and joyful by turns, by the changes of scene, by the beauty and richness of the costumes, by the *coups de théâtre*, and by the strangeness of the mimes and the dancers, he had forgotten himself to the extent of laughing, crying bravo and clapping his hands.

Entirely entered into the magic of the performance, his singular neighbors, with their mechanical cries and applause, had scarcely preoccupied him. He remembered them when the curtain fell; he saw them, during the peroration of the orchestra, get up one after another, turn left, slide as far as Milady, salute her and disappear through the door, as they had come. When the orchestra struck the last chords of the *tutti*, only the actors of the soirée's first scene remained in the room. Rear-Admiral Chalmers got up in his turn, shook his son-in-law's hand and left. Henry Smith, John Barclay, esquire and the venerable Sir Norton did not take long to follow his example. Standing and surrounded by his daughter, Miss Anna and Mistress Ingram, Milady received the bonsoir of her husband. Baron de Sarcus ran to her, seized a hand that she abandoned willingly, and said to her:

"Oh, Milady, ideal woman, marvel of grace, model of fidelity and discretion, permit me to kiss your hand."

In response. Milady jabbered a few foreign syllables, in which the baron had no difficulty in detecting a line from Sophocles:

"Go then, if you must, but remember . . ."

The chandeliers were extinguished one by one. Everything returned to the initial noise of cogwheels, which had struck the major's guests to begin with. Several times, Monsieur de Sarcus, having run out of praise and admiration, had manifested the intention to withdraw. Strange sounds suddenly struck his ears; the voice of a parrot, which seemed to be coming from the ground floor, began to whistle: "Long live Henri IV! Long live the valiant king . . ."

A little snigger escaped the major's lips

"What does that signify?" cried Monsieur de Sarcus, stupefied.

"Let's go downstairs Messieurs," replied the major, tranquilly. "You appear to be fearful for my riches; my walls seem to you to be easy to surmount, my doors easy to force. Let's go downstairs. A fortunate chance is taking charge of answering for me."

They went down. At the foot of the staircase, the major, instead of leading them into the garden right away, asked them to follow him to the left and to penetrate with him into a room whose door stood ajar. The darkness therein was profound. Scarcely had they entered than sighs alerted their attention.

Twenty gas jets suddenly illuminated a scene that astonished them at first, but soon excited their gaiety.

To the left of the entrance, in the corner of a room full of precious furniture, in front of an immense strong-box with both battens open, a poorly dressed man was standing, who was wailing. They could only see his back and could not imagine why the wretch, without being alarmed by the sound or the light, was not thinking even of withdrawing his hands, plunged into the safe.

The major invited them to approach. They understood then why the unknown man was standing still. His wrists were blue-tinted under the pressure of iron bracelets, and his hands, stretched by the torture, were suspended piteously over several piles of gold and silver arranged in battle order on the shelves.

"Aha, my lad!" said Monsieur de Sarcus, gaily. "It was a bad idea you had to attack His Excellency's guineas."

Those words were greeted by a general hilarity. The thief kept quiet. He was young, with long brown hair falling in disorder over his shoulders. His face thinned by privations, did not lack nobility or charm; his forehead shone with intelligence; the wings of his aquiline nose announced an extreme sensitivity; his mouth and chin disappeared under the waves of a silky beard; a distressing sorrow flowed from his large blue eyes.

Soon freed from the handcuffs that were martyrizing him, he bowed his head ashamedly before those who were examining him.

"How is it," the baron suddenly said to him, severely, "that a young man with your distinguished features has not recoiled before an attempted theft?"

"Alas," replied the poor devil, with an air of irresistible candor, "I wasn't thinking of stealing; I was seeking shelter."

"That's surprising," exclaimed Monsieur de Sarcus. "You have no profession, then?"

"Pardon me," stammered the wretch, in a low voice, blushing. "I'm a poet . . ."

At that confession the major and his guests looked at one another in amazement.

"A poet!" said Monsieur de Sarcus, finally. "A poet! The unfortunate fellow! They still exist, then! Oh, Milord, for the curiosity of the fact, let's call it quits and let him go."

"Mercy, Monsieur, pity!" said the tearful poet, immediately. "I beg you with joined hands not to throw me out! Where would I go? I have no shelter and no bread; put me in prison!"

The first movement of Lord Whittington, at that plea, was to take a pile of gold from the shelves of the strong-box and put it in the young man's hands. Stimulated by that example, Monsieur de Sarcus, stung by honor, plunged his hand into his fob pocket and pulled out a few silver coins, which he added to the major's gift. The poet changed color; by turns he became pale, green, and red. He opened large haggard eyes; his hands remained open; he evidently thought that he was dreaming, or the victim of a cruel trick.

"Take it, take it!" said the major, generously, "and correct yourself; embrace a career."

Monsieur de Sarcus shook his head dubiously.

The young poet seemed anxious to prove him right; convinced that he was not asleep, that he had the gold, and that he was free, he was gripped by an intoxication neighboring delirium.

"Thank you, Messieurs, thank you!" he cried suddenly, with enthusiasm. "You're noble hearts! Posterity shall know it. Thanks to you, I shall finally be able to devote myself to the composition of my odes to the moon."

"What did I tell you?" said Monsieur de Sarcus, looking at the major significantly. "Incorrigible! Incorrigible!"

The poet did not hear. Full of joy, he had already disappeared into the shadows of the night.

"That incident, Messieurs," said the major, "makes me think that the roads are not safe. Permit me to offer each of you an overcoat of my invention."

He unhooked bearskin cloaks from the wall, on the fur of which the barrels of pistols and the blades of daggers were symmetrically arranged, and invited his guests to put them on.

"Take note of the three olives lined up at the place of the heart," the major added; "the first arms the engine, the second activates it, the third puts it in repose."

Monsieur de Sarcus, and the two young secretaries, following his example, moved the first olive; the blades and gun-barrels stood up in a threatening manner. One might have thought it the back of a porcupine on the defensive.

"In case of a bad encounter," the major continued, "It will be sufficient for you to press the second olive; twenty bullets and twenty dagger-thrusts will immediately rid you of your enemies. I call this garment the infernal cloak. Please keep them in memory of me."

The baron muttered confused thanks. He put himself entirely at His Excellency's discretion, and expressed how proud and glad he would be to be agreeable to him in one way or another.

"It is presumable," said the major, as he showed his guests out, "that my neighbor will have reason to complain again more than once, and will not fail to do so. Be so kind, if possible, as to inspire a little patience in him; my neighborhood won't inconvenience him much longer, and I hold honorable functions in reserve to indemnify him for his insomnias . . ."

Monsieur de Sarcus insisted that His Excellency should not take any notice of the petit bourgeois.

"Adieu. Messieurs," said Lord Whittington with that, "adieu! May science and progress bring you joy. Before long, you'll have news of me . . ."

The unhappy bourgeois did not, in fact, take long to return to the Palais de Justice to make his complaints heard; he was gradually getting the habit of it. He and his wife were visibly perishing. He was sent away, initially with benevolence, then rather coldly, and soon rudely; the procureur général finally decided to forbid him his office door. The unfortunate fellow had recourse to petitions; they were thrown in the waste paper bin. The last one, however, was menacing:

We have come, it was said therein, *to desire a prompt death in order to be delivered as soon as possible of an existence henceforth poisoned and intolerable, Beware, Monsieur le Magistrat! Unless you put an end rapidly to the conspiracy of which we are victims, you will have to reproach yourself for the premature end of two excellent beings, models of all the virtues, who still cannot believe themselves unworthy of a happiness bought with twenty years of commerce, order, economy, privations and good housekeeping . . .*

These sinister previsions only found insensible hearts.

The good bourgeois no longer took counsel from anything but his despair. *Ab irato*,[1] he immediately fixed to his garden gate the following notice:

*Comfortable house for immediate sale,
by reason of decease.*

---

1 "By one who is angry."

A buyer presented himself. The contract of sale was promptly drawn up; it only lacked the signatures. One terrible night changed the dispositions of the honest proprietor unexpectedly.

It might have been an hour after midnight. By the scintillating light of the stars, nature was in repose. Dull rumbles troubled the silence of the plain at intervals; one might have thought that a storm was approaching, or that an earthquake was threatened. Gradually, the rumbles increased in intensity and became formidable; nothing similar had been heard before; there was no rain or wind; the din, without being reminiscent of thunder, was more horrible; it was a singular mixture of a thousand uncomfortable sounds, a gathering, at a single point, of all the noisy métiers of the entire world. At that game, Vulcan and his cyclopes, working in concert under the sonorous vaults of Etna, would have admitted themselves vanquished.

For about two hours, it seemed that millions of hammers, millions of files and millions of saws, confounded with as many factory bellows and whistles, were beating, filing, tapping and sawing iron bars, sheet metal, wood and stone at the same time. That giant, monstrous, terrible symphony was followed by an explosion that caused the houses to vacillate for two leagues around and bore fear into the hearts of the most intrepid; many people thought that their last hour was nigh.

Nevertheless, that was all. A mortal silence followed . . .

In the morning, the poor bourgeois, half dead with fear, took the risk of looking out of the window. What he perceived made him believe that he was not really awake. He rubbed his eyes. No mistake was possible. A few seconds of astonishment nailed him to the spot and paralyzed him. Shortly afterwards he ran to his wife, and, mute with the force of emotion, drew her by the skirt to the window. His wife was no less profoundly astounded.

Instead of the high and somber walls that had masked their view the day before, a beautiful golden gate presently embraced a vast square, in the center of which stood a monument of sorts.

The man and the woman, soon at the foot of that grille, did not take long to join their conjectures with those of the crowd that was gathering incessantly before that miraculous transformation.

At the head of the alerted authorities, Monsieur de Sarcus arrived later, in whose memory the prophetic last words of the major resonated once again: "Before long, you'll have news of me . . ." He cleaved through the groups, penetrated into the garden and marched straight to the monument.

It was a grandiose and bizarre mausoleum. Ten pages would not suffice to give the details of its composition. Its form was impossible to describe. On its granite base reposed a gigantic group skillfully conceived, in which one distinguished, among a thousand other things, a locomotive, an aerostat, a ship, electric cables, helices and telescopes. The ensemble was dominated by a little pyramid and a lightning-conductor. On two of the four faces of the pedestal, a marble plaque awaited inscriptions.

On one side, the entrance to a cellar opened in the base. Monsieur Sarcus had torches brought, and descended bravely. Twenty steps conducted him to a vast hall sustained by pillars and buttresses. Along the walls, heaps of manuscripts and several cupboards were arranged in an orderly manner, while in the center there was a marble tomb. The baron approached it; thick unsilvered glass covered it. Through the crystal, Monsieur de Sarcus perceived the major lying on his back; he was clad in his red coat and coiffed in his hat with cock's plumes; apart from his head, which was entirely visible, the rest of his body was plunged in soft cushions. It seemed that a thin layer of wax was spread over his features. One of his hands was holding a scroll of paper.

Monsieur de Sarcus ordered his men to lift the lid of the tomb. The scroll of paper was addressed to him; it contained the expression of Lord Whittington's desires.

One could not say that it was a testament.

I am not dead. Life is simply suspended in me by an anesthesia of my invention.

Thus the major began. He continued:

The recipe will be found among my papers. I desire to see with my own eyes the world in sixty years. To dissimulate nothing, in the very bosom of my unalterable happiness, a certain malaise slyly germinated and prospered, something comparable to ennui or spleen. Suicide would have delivered me from it, if I had not had the resource of going to sleep.

During the next sixty years someone might have found a remedy for the tapeworm before the development of which all my discoveries have thus far failed. That is the question. My neighbor, during his life, should be charged with guarding my body in return for twenty pounds sterling per month; it is a sinecure, the privilege of which I bequeath to him with the intention of enabling him to forget my turbulent neighborhood. His task will consist of dusting me from time to time and renewing the layer of wax over my face once a year. He will choose his successor himself among the honest men of his acquaintance. After sixty years, the person who finds himself constituted my guardian in that fashion will observe scrupulously the instructions consigned in my papers, in order to recall me to life.

Following a number of other dispositions, the major added:

All the manuscripts in the cellar should be confided to the care of the members of the Académie des Sciences, who should be kind enough to appoint a commission to put them in order, annotate them, publish them and aid with all their influence the popularization of my discoveries. In addition, those messieurs are requested to deign to found an annual prize of eight hundred pounds sterling to the benefit of the person who discovers a means of being perfectly happy when dolor comes to be radically abolished. In the presence of the incurable wellbeing with which science, the industrial arts, mechanics and drainage threaten to endow humankind, that foundation appears to me to be essentially philanthropic . . .

I bequeath to the Académie des Sciences, as a mark of my profound admiration and high esteem, a perpetual income of eight thousand pounds sterling, to be divided annually between the forty armchairs of the section. Half of the sixty millions contained in banknotes in my cupboards will suffice amply, I hope, for these various legacies.

The honorable mission of supervising the rigorous accomplishment of those express desires was conferred to the good will and intelligence of Baron de Sarcus.

That news produced a prolonged sensation in the scholarly world. Various periodicals, including the *Journal of Practical Mechanics*, appeared framed in black for several months. A commission was immediately appointed to coordinate, examine and explore the major's papers. At the innumerable marvels of which they contained the seed, the members of the sciences section of the Académie were seized by an extraordinary enthusiasm. They got up as one man and went in procession, in formal costume, to the dwelling of Lord Whittington.

By their cares, on one side of the pedestal was engraved in golden letters:

TO THE SCIENTIFIC MESSIAH

And on the other:

THERE IS NO OTHER GOD THAN MAN
AND WHITTINGTON IS HIS PROPHET

So be it!

Romanzoff

I

ON a cold November day in 1841, at one o'clock in the afternoon, a man enveloped in a hooded cloak arrived outside a house in the Rue Monsieur-le-Prince and darted a rapid glance over the rental notices that were balanced over the door.

He went into the concierge's lodge.

"Madame," he said to the woman who was there, "You have apartments to let?"

"Yes, Monsieur, one on the third and another on the first."

"Would you care to show me the one on the first?"

The concierge, immediately seduced by the voice, the manners and the face of the young man, took the keys in haste and went upstairs before him.

He was of average height; his pale face had distinction; his blue eyes were very soft; a long blond beard hid the lower part of his face; his accent betrayed a man of the North.

Without paying much attention, he went through the various rooms of the apartment, asked the price, and rented it. The apartment was empty, he could move in immediately.

"My name is Romanzoff," he said, as he departed. "If you want to obtain references, go to see my notary, Monsieur H****, in the Rue ****, number **."

The name and address of the notary were there. But what was the point? In the course of the day, suppliers brought a full set of beautiful furniture for Monsieur Romanzoff worth far more than the best references. After that, the concierge thought she could dispense with obtaining information on the subject of her new tenant. In any case, as her own words were to testify later, she would have accepted the man on his good appearance.

Monsieur Romanzoff had a manner of living that immediately caused him to be taken for an eccentric. He lived absolutely alone, did not receive anyone, did not go out—or very rarely, and then only in the evening.

In the early days, he went out two or three times, at the most, in the morning, to go to the market. He was seen to return each time followed by a commissionaire whose back was curbed under a basket full of meat, vegetables and wine; all those provisions were deposited in a cellar, from which Romanzoff took every day what he needed to nourish himself.

None of those who laid eyes on him could conceive that a well-educated man, who occupied an apartment of more than two thousand francs and had rich furniture, mirrors and carpets, lived in that fashion. It was all the stranger because, far from being a miser, he always had money to hand, and paid for everything without haggling.

The concierge proposed to him one day that she procure him a housekeeper.

"It's not worth the trouble," he replied. "There's very little to do in my home; everything there is in order and I don't disturb anything. In any case," he added, "I'm expecting a young man, who will aid me if necessary."

Indeed, a few days later, the announced young man arrived. He was a Wurtemburger named Pressel, who said that he was working with a view to obtaining a diploma in architecture.

From that day on, Romanzoff ceased entirely to go out in the morning; the care of going to the market and buying provisions there was exclusively a matter for Pressel.

The young man had difficulty expressing himself in French; he only spoke about Romanzoff, whom he called his benefactor, with respect and enthusiasm.

"Although very rich and of a grand family," he said, in his half-German, half-French jargon, "he is the simplest and the best of men. He only has two passions: studying and doing good. I can't tell you how much I owe him already. In exchange for services without importance, he lodges me, nourishes me, dresses me, buys me books, gives me lessons and enables me to follow a course in architecture. He only wants to send me back to my homeland when I've entirely concluded my studies."

These details excited more interest than surprise; they simply corroborated the idea of Romanzoff already formed. His sensibility was evidently excessive; any poverty caused him to vibrate and overexcited him. Under the influence of that sensibility, giving alms was for him a practice that seemed necessary to the tranquility of his life. It frequently happened that he attracted to his antechamber a few of those petty chimney-sweeps who are always so hungry, at least in appearance, whom he stuffed with bread and meat, or barefoot children in rags, to whom, after having interrogated them at length, he gave old clothes and undergarments, and often even money.

And certainly, in all of that, ostentation only played a very effaced role; he imposed it as a duty, on those on whom he had compassion to be discreet, not to talk about him, under any pretext.

His life never ceased to be narrowly confined. The interior of his apartment was like a harem; apart from Pressel, no one went in there. He did not receive any letters, he went for entire weeks without going out; if he did go out, it was only in the evening, at dusk, not to return, for the most part, until four or five days later.

Only once did the concierge penetrate his home, in the morning, in order to darn a rip in a carpet. That woman, a middle-aged widow named Madame Delte, adored Romanzoff. It was only with a profound emotion that she entered the sanctuary of her idol.

Sitting at a vast table on which mathematical instruments, a guitar, books and papers were scattered, Romanzoff was giving Pressel a lesson in calculus. In spite of her emotion, the good woman, without pausing in her darning, darted furtive glances to either side. She felt a chill in her bones on perceiving that Romanzoff's vivid, penetrating blue eyes were stubbornly fixed on her.

One day, a woman came to see him. Although very simply dressed, she was not without elegance. The thickness of a veil hid her face rigorously. She asked whether Monsieur Romanzoff was at home, and on what floor he lived. After that—for she came again from time to time, always veiled with the same care—she went past the lodge and went upstairs without turning her head. That woman's visits had a mysterious character that added further to the increasing curiosity that Romanzoff excited.

II

The house of five or six stories, grouped in the same column of air people of very different professions. They included young people, students, painters or men of letters, who frequently met up on the ground floor, in the concierge's lodge, where they held discussions of a sort, on trivial matters. Women from the house or the neighborhood sometimes swelled those meetings. In Romanzoff's absence, Pressel came there to pass the time and listen open-mouthed to discussions that he did not always understand.

Two or three times, Romanzoff appeared there unexpectedly, and stayed for a few moments. People talked about him incessantly, and only saw him rarely; he could not fail to acquire a great prestige. By coming to sit down familiarly in the lodge, he proved that, if he refused liaisons, it was not out of pride. The sensation that he produced every time was vivid. Indiscreet individuals, without intending any malice, submitted him to a sort of examination there. He could speak several languages, had a thorough knowledge of history, philosophy and mathematics, and his opinions on music and painting attested a veritable intelligence of those arts; but it was about political economics, above all, that he chatted most willingly. As soon as there was a question of pauperism, his eyes glittered, his eloquence caught fire, and his pantomime acquired a singular vivacity.

Later, they were to recall, not without amazement, having heard remarks of this sort emerging from his mouth:

"I don't believe that there is only injustice down here—in the division of wealth, for example, which we attribute to hazard, there is probably more equity than we generally suppose. However, to all evidence, too many people dispose of a fortune far superior to the moderation of their appetites, and to the resources of their faculties, and among our wounds, that is doubtless one of the most serious."

To hear Romanzoff, even the least miserly among the latter, hoarding and withdrawing from circulation innumerable riches, were like people who spent their leisure damming a river and amassing water in the depths of a gulf. He added: "If people once consented to see and to desire it, half of the miseries that desolate humankind would disappear from the world tomorrow without a blow being struck and without the slightest perturbation."

His speech, like his life, had something enigmatic and tenebrous about it. Flashes sometimes traversed that obscurity. For instance: "Poverty is superfluous in this world. When it has disappeared, enough dolors will still remain to the poor human species."

These fragments, if they are not absolutely textual, at least give the exact hue of the sentiments that Romanzoff had, or by which he wanted people to believe that he was animated.

Let us add that he addressed himself to young people and that he sometimes spoke with passion and vehemence, as when, to cite only one example, he cried: "Oh, the Pharisees, the Pharisees! Still the same, after eighteen centuries. Whited sepulchers, full of bones! The Gospel is to recommence. We shall see! From this excess of disorders and evils, perhaps some good will emerge."

That suffices to explain the enthusiasm that he succeeded in exciting in the souls of some of those who listened to him.

At other times, when he dared to speak ill of "actors of sensibility" who only had, unfortunately, sterile tears and honeyed words, he said on that subject:

"I deem that we have the right to be made of bronze with our fellows, and that it would be at least indiscreet, apart from what laws and usages, to impose on humans anything whatsoever. But if, with the decision to dismiss a wretch, one wants to deceive him as to the intentions one nourishes in his regard, if, with the heart of a prison guard, one aspires to the reputation of a sensitive man and the benefits of that reputation, that seems to me to be hateful, and worthy of criticism."

If he said that, if he even emphasized it strangely, it can be seen, by means of two examples chosen from among twenty, that, according to all appearances, his penchant disposed him to action as well as speech.

III

On entering the house, the lodge was to the right and the staircase straight ahead. Under the stairwell, next to the lodge, the cellar opened. The widow Delte slept on the entresol. Between her bedroom and the lodge, in the wall of the staircase, there was a low cavity, irregular but large, deep and enclosed, which served Madame Delte as a lumber-room.

One morning, Romanzoff, going down from his apartment to the cellar, overheard sighs in passing that were coming from the door of that obscure and airless niche. He slipped into the lodge immediately.

"I'm doubtless mistaken," Madame, he said, with some astonishment. "No one lodges in such a place; the plaints that I heard as I came down were only an illusion."

"What plaints. Monsieur Romanzoff?"

"It seemed to me that they were coming from that cupboard fitted into the wall alongside your bedroom."

"I know; a poor woman . . ."

"A poor woman!" Romanzoff interrupted, swiftly.

No one contests that charity, in France, especially in the big cities, is exercised abundantly, in a thousand forms, with spontaneity, discretion and an entirely exemplary simplicity. Those who are suffering enjoy a kind of right to it. Nevertheless, many more miseries, for want of being seen, and for want of being divined, are not assisted. It is the exception, but it was the present case.

It was a matter of a young woman, devoid of family and friends, or at least only having relatives and friends impotent to aid her. Everything suggests that even advice was lacking.

Her husband, a laborious worker, had fallen ill six or seven months after their marriage. Flattering himself that he would soon be cured, he had yielded to the pleas of his wife, who did not want to see him transported to a hospice. The result of that was a state of frightful deprivation. A series of disastrous expedients had burdened the future without determining a less somber present. Moving from crisis to crisis, the worker had died, leaving his wife pregnant and about to give birth.

Overwhelmed by debts, devoid of resources, credit and hope, nothing remained for her but to solicit admission to the Bourbe.[1] She had entered it exhausted by fatigue and privations, and had brought into the world a child who had only lived for a few hours. Her

---

1 "La Bourbe" was a familiar term for the Hôpital de la Maternité in Paris; its literal meaning, tellingly, is "the Mire."

condition of fever and exhaustion required long rest and great care, but a hospice is not a sanitarium; she had to leave and yield her place to another.

A furnished room at six francs a month had seen her labor doggedly for a few days, but her strength had betrayed her courage. To complete the disaster it had been necessary, at the demand of the landlord, to quit the corner of an attic where she took shelter.

In the evening, in the cold, half mad with despair, she had wandered through the streets, staggering, uniquely sustained by the dread of being accused of vagabondage and arrested. An inspiration had finally taken her to the Rue Monsieur-le-Prince, to the home of the concierge, whom she had known for a long time, and the latter, touched by compassion, had offered her, while awaiting something better, a camp-bed in the rat-hole of sorts from which Romanzoff had just heard groans emerging.

"They say that heaven helps those who help themselves," added Madame Delte, in conclusion, "but it's necessary, Monsieur Romanzoff, that one has the strength to help oneself."

Romanzoff was moved, beside himself. "Is it possible?" he said. "The poor woman! Why didn't you tell me right away?"

"She's only been here since yesterday evening."

"Finally! Finally!" said Romanzoff. "God be praised! It's Providence that has guided her here. Wait!"

With that, Romanzoff went out abruptly and went upstairs to his apartment. He came down again a few minutes later.

"Madame," he said, putting a hundred francs in the hands of the concierge, "this is the money that you'll give to the poor woman. Let her find lodgings and re-cover her health. Be kind enough to keep me informed of her needs. I'll take charge of everything until she can find work. Only I beg you not to tell her where this money comes from."

He took advantage of the amazement that action caused the concierge to withdraw.

IV

Since his entry to the house, which went back to the month of November 1841, Romanzoff had marked al-most every day by some act of generosity. Many people were beginning to weary of hearing the man praised perpetually, and willingly lent an ear to certain mockers courageous enough to turn his benevolence to ridicule. Others, in whom Romanzoff had stimulated a curios-ity akin to passion, murmured at the memory of the mystery with which he stubbornly surrounded his life. Gradually, indiscretion, jealousy, slander and injustice conspired against him and laid siege, in a manner of speaking, to his individuality. All in all, none of those hostile sentiments succeeded in inspiring a conjecture capable of lasting even a few hours.

The sixth of January 1842 arrived. That day was to be epoch-making in the house.

Romanzoff was absent. Between two and three o'clock in the afternoon a young woman came to ask for him.

"He's not in, Mademoiselle," replied Madame Delte.

"Do you think he'll return soon?"

"I hope so, and if you'd care to wait . . ."

The young woman sat down. She might have been twenty-five years old. Her physiognomy respired honesty; her attire was very simple.

Nothing concerning Monsieur Romanzoff was indifferent to Madame Delte. The desire to know what he might have in common with that young woman soon caused her to break the ice. She entered gradually into conversation regarding her tenant, and spoke about him with an enthusiasm that came from the heart.

"Oh, Madame," said the young woman, emotionally, "say everything good you wish about Monsieur Romanzoff; I have reason to believe that he is even more generous than you suppose."

A kind of intimacy was rapidly established between the two women. Thanks to Monsieur Romanzoff, the moments passed rapidly for her. The young woman finally seemed to be unable to wait any longer.

"Would you like me to give him a message?" Madame Delte asked.

"I alone can tell him what I feel," replied the young woman. "Gratitude is overflowing in my soul. If you knew . . . !" She paused, and then said: "Look, Madame, you love Monsieur Romanzoff, and it's bad to hide a secret from you that will complete your knowledge of him and redouble your admiration . . ."

The father of the young women kept a restaurant in the Les Halles quarter. He was a former soldier and seemingly the most confident of men; numerous disappointments had not cured him of granting credit to all comers, and he had always lacked the courage to pursue his creditors legally. Ten years of that disinterest, spent in the midst of alarms and perpetual embarrassment, had finally determined his ruination.

Romanzoff had sat down at the worthy man's table for a long time; although he had ceased to eat there, he continued nevertheless to go to see him from time to time. Recently, in one of those visits, Romanzoff, struck by the bleak expression with which the old soldier had postponed payment of a bill, had taken him aside and constrained him to admit the disorder of his affairs.

"How much do you need?" he asked him thereafter.

"Let's not talk about that," replied the old man, shaking his head. "It's pointless."

"Tell me anyway."

"I'd need at least seven or eight thousand francs. I'm doomed."

"Perhaps not," Romanzoff replied. "My personal resources evidently don't permit me to lend you that sum, but I know rich and charitable individuals who probably wouldn't refuse you their aid, on my recommendation. Hope!"

He left.

"His good heart was known to us," the young woman added. "In spite of that, Madame, to speak frankly, we didn't found much hope on what he said. How could one flatter oneself, in fact, on finding such a large sum without any guarantee? The next day, however, a young man placed in my father's hands a package sealed with the grandeur of a letter. We didn't know what to think. The young man only came in and left again. Imagine our surprise, our joy and our transport when, the envelope having been opened, eight thousand-franc banknotes fell out. We couldn't believe our eyes. For me, especially, Madame, it was more than salvation, it was my father's life. For want of having books in order, he could have done worse than go bankrupt, and perhaps he wouldn't have had the courage to survive that shame . . ."

Amazed herself, and transported by admiration, Madame Delte agreed that that further example far outstripped what she already knew about Monsieur Romanzoff.

"I laughed," said the young woman, "I wept, I gesticulated like a madwoman. The need to express my gratitude tormented me more than a fever. But he didn't appear! Unable to stand it, I've run here; he gave us this address himself . . ."

The young woman paused again, and added as she stood up: "But he isn't coming. A longer absence would make my father anxious. I'm going. Don't fail to tell him, I beg you Madame, that we want to see him and that, if he doesn't want to be persecuted, it's absolutely necessary for him to yield to our pleas . . ."

Madame Delte promised not to forget the recommendation, and with that assurance, the young woman hastened to depart.

V

Having gone out together one evening, Romanzoff and Pressel had given no sign of life for at least a week. It was not habitual for them to be absent for so long. Madame Delte expected to see one or other of them appear at any moment. The visit she had just received, in adding to her enthusiasm for Romanzoff, made her wish for his return with an exceptional impatience.

Under the empire of that impatience, at about eight o'clock in the evening, two violent blows of the door-knocker caused her to shudder with pleasure.

It was, in fact, her tenant.

He entered, or, to put it better, irrupted into her lodge.

Enveloped, as always, in his burnoose, as pale as a corpse, with sweat on his brow and haggard eyes, he was at grips with a convulsive tremor that he was trying in vain to dominate.

"Madame, Madame," he said, in a breathless voice, "quickly, fetch someone . . . I need to watch over a friend who is dangerously ill. I want to get some books from my apartment and I don't know what has become of my key . . ."

Romanzoff's plea respired such anxiety that Madame Delte, neglecting what she had to say, hastened to do as he asked. She ran to the locksmith, and soon returned to announce that the workman was following her.

But it was the sixth of January, the day of the Epiphany; the locksmith, who was eating a celebration cake with his family, forgot or did not hurry to come.

144

Still as pale and as agitated, inattentive to the words of Madame Delte, who, to pass the time, carried out the commission with which the young woman had charged her, Romanzoff paced back and forth. He seemed to be hesitant to ask the good woman to return to the workman's house, but he sometimes looked at her with an expression that was a thousand times more eloquent than any prayer.

Madame Delte understood. This time, the locksmith came with her. He was a stout and grave man who looked as if he were coming to certify a decease. Romanzoff seized a candle and went up rapidly before him.

"Hurry, please," he said.

Insensible to that excitement, the fat man, with a sullen expression, examined the lock slowly and got ready to try, one after another, the skeleton keys with which he was equipped.

That slowness put Romanzoff to the torture.

"I don't have a moment to lose!" he cried, in an irresistible tone. "Quickly, dear Monsieur! If necessary, break the lock!"

Already discontented by having been extracted from his family joys, the locksmith, who thought that his presence alone testified to a generosity worthy of admiration, found the imperious tone in which Romanzoff was speaking to him entirely inappropriate. He redoubled his slowness and awkwardness.

"Please, Monsieur!" added Romanzoff, in a voice vibrant with devouring anguish.

"Well, Monsieur," replied the locksmith, incapable of hiding his ill-humor any longer, "this lock is very difficult, and I only have keys. It was necessary to tell me to bring a crowbar."

Meanwhile, he stood up, and gave evidence of a desire to beat a retreat.

"I beg you, Monsieur!" said Romanzoff, barring his passage resolutely. "One of my friends is dying; I need to get my lancets in order to bleed him. Every moment that goes past increases the danger and my despair. Perhaps I'll arrive too late."

Romanzoff's expression, tone and words finally moved the locksmith to greater urgency. He set to work again eagerly; his zeal did the trick. "We're there!" he said, almost immediately.

The door ceded. Romanzoff hurtled into his apartment like a torrent through a breach. After staying there for three or four minutes, at the most, he reappeared, hiding one or more objects of considerable volume under his cloak, and without paying any heed to his open door he went downstairs precipitately.

Madame Delte was on the threshold of her lodge.

"Adieu, Madame!" said Romanzoff, swiftly.

"So, Monsieur Romanzoff," the concierge hastened to say, "it's agreed that I shan't wait up for you this evening?"

"I'll come back . . . at two o'clock," stammered Romanzoff. "Adieu, Madame," he added, pressing her hands. "We'll see one another again."

Then he disappeared.

VI

In the evenings, Madame Delte did not quit the ground floor before having seen all the tenants of the house who usually made her wait longest return. Her vigil was rarely prolonged beyond midnight. Then she closed her lodge, turned the key twice in the door to the street, and went up to her bedroom. From that moment on, if, by chance, someone knocked, the good woman had to get out of bed and go downstairs to open up.

Two o'clock, two o'clock, she thought. *Is that two o'clock in the morning or two o'clock in the afternoon? No matter,* she added, *I'll wait until two o'clock in the morning, just in case.*

That was, in any case, something that cost her little, since it was a matter of "the good Monsieur Romanzoff."

Those tenants of the house who had gone out returned successively. Midnight chimed, then one o'clock, and then two o'clock, and Monsieur Romanzoff did not appear. Finally convinced that he would not return, Madame Delte locked her door and went up to her bedroom.

She had gone to bed and had just put out her lamp when three blows of the knocker shook the door to the street.

Ah! the good woman said to herself. *There's Monsieur Romanzoff.*

She leapt out of bed, put on a skirt and, without relighting her lamp for fear of making her tenant wait, she hastened to go downstairs in the dark.

"Is that you, Monsieur Romanzoff?" she asked.

A voice replied affirmatively.

She turned the key in the door and opened the door by a crack. The batten was pushed from outside with such violence that Madame Delte nearly fell backwards. At the same time she heard a confused noise of footsteps and respirations, and saw, by the light of a nearby gas-lamp projected through the open door, several human silhouettes pass by. Paralyzed by fear, the poor woman thought that it was a gang of assassins and that her last hour was nigh.

Feeling, in the darkness—for the door had been closed again—that she was being crowded and jostled by men whose number was magnified by her fear, she only thought of asking for mercy.

"Messieurs, messieurs," she stammered, "don't hurt me."

"Shut up, shut up!" someone said, in a low voice, trying to close her mouth.

"My God, my God, Messieurs, don't hurt me!" she repeated, while making efforts to free herself.

"Once again, shut up!" said several voices. "And give us a light; no one will do you any harm."

Half-suffocated, tittering, she went back to her bedroom, wondering whether she ought to shout for help. It seemed wiser to keep quiet and obey, so she lit her lamp, dressed in haste, and went downstairs.

A dozen men, clad in hoods, with cravats over their noses, appeared to be consulting one another. They formed a circle around a man who had a red ribbon in his buttonhole. The external appearance of the men reassured Madame Delte slightly. The decorated man detached himself from the group and approached her.

"On what floor does Romanzoff live?" he demanded, in an imperative tone.

"On the first."

"Is he at home?"

"No, Monsieur."

"When did you last see him?"

"Yesterday evening."

"At what time?"

"Eight o'clock. He came in and went out almost immediately."

"Is he coming back?"

"Yes, Monsieur, at two o'clock."

"Two o'clock in the morning?"

"He didn't tell me that, Monsieur. I thought it was him when you knocked."

"How's that?"

Madame Delte told him then, in the slightest detail, what had happened the previous evening between herself and Monsieur Romanzoff.

"That's good," replied the man with the red ribbon. "We'll wait. Open your lodge and go back to your bedroom."

No doubt was now possible regarding the estate of those men and their commission. At daybreak, one of them went out and returned shortly afterwards accompanied by a new individual. They all went up to the first floor together, went into Romanzoff's apartment, which was still open, and proceeded with a scrupulous search, which resulted in the seizure of a multitude of items.

What had Monsieur Romanzoff done? Of what crime was he accused? Everything encouraged the belief that the greatest importance was attached to his capture. A conspiracy was the unique misdeed with which anyone in the house dared to tarnish the memory of that generous individual. At any rate, the mystery would not be cleared up for some time. Not a single word that escaped from the mouth of the agents furnished a clue in that regard. After remaining in Monsieur Romanzoff's apartment for more than an hour, they left, except for two who were left on sentry duty in the lodge.

Those two men installed themselves comfortably and, inviting the concierge to pay no attention to them and to be discreet, they observed in silence the people who went out and those who came in. At dinner time, one of them went up to Romanzoff's apartment and came down shortly afterwards with bread, cold meat, labeled wine, etc. Madame Delte hastened to furnish them with places at table, and they ate without taking their eyes off the door, as tranquilly as they would have done in their own homes.

No other incident occurred that day. The next day, the lodge was occupied by two other agents, who, after a day and a night of service, were replaced by two others—and so on, for eight or ten days. They went away one morning, no longer to reappear. Nevertheless, from time to time, during the day or in the evening, strangers came to ask for Monsieur Romanzoff. Madame Delte had to pay with many anxieties for the honor of having known such an amiable tenant.

She had, moreover, been summoned to the Palais de Justice, to the study of an examining magistrate, and there she had to submit to a long interrogation regarding the habits, the work and the relations of Monsieur Romanzoff. The honest woman only knew the details previously recorded; she would have liked nothing better than to learn something more, but she was dismissed without the slightest satisfaction of her ardent curiosity. No hero had ever floated, in her eyes, in a more romantic atmosphere, or inspired a more violent interest.

One morning, the postman handed her the following letter:

> *Dear Mother,*
> *Unfortunate circumstances have accidentally closed the door of a prison on me. Don't be afflicted, any more than I am frightened myself. Innocent and full of confidence in the law, I hope to be released very soon. In the meantime, the deprivation of underwear and other objects of toilette is*

making me suffer greatly. The totality of my possessions remain in Monsieur Romanzoff's apartment. I have been permitted to ask you for them in writing. You will find the list below. If you would be good enough to put it all in a parcel and have it sent to me at Sainte-Pélagie, where I am detained, you would be rendering me a service that I will never forget.

> *Your respectful and devoted son,*
> *Pressel.*

The reading of that letter threw Madame Delte into the grip of new perplexities. Alarmed without knowing why, vaguely fearing being compromised in some plot, she came gradually no longer to be able to sleep tranquilly. The conjectures of the women of the neighborhood finished turning her mind upside-down. The letter surprised her in the most forceful of her anxieties. She really did not know what to do. Someone finally advised her to go to the parquet and put the letter in the hands of the magistrate who had questioned her. That is what she did.

Having read the piece of paper, the examining magistrate asked Madame Delte what the expression "dear mother" signified, which figured at the head of the letter. Madame Delte was quite unable to resolve the question. She was no less astonished by the term than the judge. There was only one way of explaining it, and it was not very explicit. It is the custom among workers linked in companionship to call the woman in whose home the live and eat, "Mother." Perhaps Pressel had been a companion; perhaps he had simply frequented companions.

In any case, the magistrate did not insist on the detail. He sent Madame Delte away, after having authorized her to do what Pressel desired.

VIII

An interval of about twenty-two months separated the ensemble of these events from the judiciary debates that were to complete and explain them. It is necessary to leap over the interval between January 1842 and October 1843. Only then, before the Court of Assizes of the Seine, was it learned what Romanzoff really was, and of what crime such an apparently commendable man was accused.

In 1841, the Prussian government had been alarmed by numerous counterfeits of its treasury bills. The examination of the forgeries testified to an extreme skill. As soon as the flaws that could reveal their falsity were identified by the newspapers, the forger or forgers hastened to correct them. After eight years and eight successive editions, they had succeeded in a despairingly exact imitation.

A special agent, Magnus von Mirbach, sent from Berlin to Paris in order to search for the author of the frauds, established that the number of false bills put in circulation amounted to between four hundred and fifty and five hundred thalers, and acquired the certainty that the forger was one Theodor Herweg, who had for an accomplice a man named Knapp, both Prussian nationals. Mirbach neglected nothing to discover them and have them arrested, but even though a reward of three thousand francs had been promised for the arrest of each of them, they were able to escape the intelligent and active research of the police.

However, a fact denounced by the English police suddenly put the law on their track.

On the thirtieth of November 1841 a young man about thirty-five years old presented himself in the office of Mr. Buttson, a London banker, and offered for exchange thirty-six thousand-franc bills of the Societé Général de Belgique, to favor industry. The young man, whose name, according to his passport, was Kaniez, declared that he was resident at the Guildhall Coffee House. Mr. Buttson took the thirty-six bills and gave him banknotes in exchange. The bills, sent to Antwerp and Brussels, proved to be fake, and were put in the hands of the king's prosecutor. It goes without saying that the so-called Kaniez had already disappeared from the Guildhall Coffee House.

Led to believe that the individual in question, who was traveling with a comrade, had headed for France, English agents monitored in Boulogne and Calais the identity of travelers who had recently passed through those two towns in order to go either from Paris to London or from London to Paris. They discovered by that means: firstly, that on the twenty-eighth of November 1841, one Charles Vongier had embarked in Calais for London, coming from Paris, bearing a

154

passport issued at the Prefecture of Police on the previous twenty-second of May, as had Ernest Dareno, also coming from Paris, bearer of a passport issued by the same prefecture on the twenty-first of June 1841; and secondly, that those same individuals had disembarked in Boulogne on the second of December, and that their disembarkation coincided with the exchange, at Adam et Cie of Boulogne, of one of the banknotes handed to Kaniez by Mr. Buttson in exchange for Belgian bills.

That was already something.

Mr. Buttson had the numbers and a description of the banknotes delivered by him to Kaniez inserted in *Galignani's*,[1] but the forgers changed the numbers and the surveillance of the money-changers of Paris was deceived.

On the other hand, on the basis of the information that had been transmitted to them by the English police, the Parisian police discovered that of the two passports that the individuals were carrying, the one dated the twenty-first of June 1841 had not been issued to a man named Ernest Dareno but to a woman who called herself Ernestine Daren. That passport had therefore been falsified.

Now, on the sixth of January 1842, the day at the decline of which the panic-stricken Romanzoff had his door opened by a locksmith, the woman Daren came to the Prefecture of Police to request a passport for

---

1 *Galignani's Messenger* was an English-language newspaper printed in Paris, launched in 1814, famous for global news coverage and progressive views. It is mentioned in many nineteenth-century novels by English writers.

Cologne. Asked whether she did not have her previous passport, she said that she did not know what had become of it. To arrest her immediately would not have been clever; accomplices might have been waiting at the door, taken umbrage at that arrest and escaped. A new passport was issued to Madame Daren, and action was limited to following her. She went to the Rue Vital in Passy, where she occupied a house between a courtyard and a garden. It was learned from neighbors that the lady lived there with a foreigner by the name of Romanzoff.

That same day, at nightfall, a police commissaire, accompanied by the chief of service of the Sûreté and several agents, introduced himself into Madame Daren's house in order to search it. Three large-caliber pistols, loaded and primed, were lying on a table in the bedroom; under the bolster of the bed a five-hundred-franc bill was hidden. In an alcove annexed to the bedroom there was a small copper-plate printing press, devoid of characters and almost new, which the woman Daren declared to be the property of a man named Romanzoff, who used it to print engravings.

"Where is this Romanzoff?" she was asked.

"He's gone out," she replied. "I'm expecting him."

At that same moment, the service-chief of the Sûreté saw a light at the back of the garden, and perceived that there was a small detached building on that side. He immediately headed toward it with his men.

The lights and the noise alerted the attention of Romanzoff, who was then in the detached building with Pressel. Romanzoff divined the danger. Without losing a second, he opened a window that overlooked a deserted back-street, threw his cloak out over the pavement, let himself slide down it, and ran precipitately to his lodgings in Paris, where the scene sketched in chapter V occurred.

Pressel was, therefore alone. He had closed the window and was sitting at a table where two places were set.

At the sight of the young man, whose beardless face did not indicate more than twenty years, the service-chief of the Sûreté understood that he did not have before his eyes either of the two forgers whose descriptions had been given to him. He questioned him. The young man stammered in poor French that his name was Pressel, that he was originally from Wurtemburg, and that he had met Monsieur Romanzoff in London, on whose invitation he had come to Paris.

"Why are there two places set on that table?" he was asked.

"I'm expecting Monsieur Romanzoff for dinner," Pressel replied.

A further search was carried out. It seemed that they were in the forger's veritable workshop. Scattered on a table were gravers, soft wax, acids, a press, proofs of fake bills and, finally, five engraved plates, four of which had evidently served not only to print fake Prussian five-thaler bills but also the fake thousand-franc bills of the Societé Générale de Belgique. Under the envelope containing the plates, thirty-six sheets of paper were found, blue-gray in color, in the middle of which, when they were held up to the light, the words "thousand francs" were legible; those sheets were doubtless destined for a further printing of Belgian bills.

Pressel was questioned again.

"Where are you staying in Paris?"

"With Monsieur Romanzoff."

"Where does he live?"

"For a few moments, Monsieur," replied Pressel, "I've been trying to remember the name of the street, but I confess to you frankly that I haven't been able to succeed."

After having searched for some time and mangled twenty street names, Pressel ended up finding the Rue Monsieur-le-Prince.

"Don't you know the number either?"

Pressel, in fact, had a no less infidel memory on that point. The hours went by. It was not far from midnight when the police finally knew that Romanzoff lived in the Rue Monsieur-le-Prince, number two. It will be remembered what happened there and poor Madame Delte's alarms.

The search of Romanzoff's domicile led to several discoveries no less important. Among other things, a passport was found issued by the Prefecture of Police on the first of April 1941 to Romanzoff of Rochum, Westphalia; a portrait made in England that was supposed, by virtue of certain indications, to be that of Romanzoff; engraving implements; material employed for the printing of proofs; twenty-one sheets of pink paper in the middle of which had been formed, by means of a stamp, the words and figures "*fünf thaler 1835*" and the interlaced letters FR.

The telegraph had sent Romanzoff's description in all directions; arrest warrants, accompanied by lithographs of the portrait found in the Rue Monsieur-le-Prince, were sent to the environs of Paris and the principal cities of France; but for two years, Romanzoff had evaded all the efforts made to capture him by the police forces of France, Prussia, England and Belgium.

IX

For want of sufficient evidence, after several months of detention in Sainte-Pélagie, Pressel had been released. Only the woman Daren, whom the accusation identified as the accomplice of the forgers, had been retained under arrest and imprisoned in Saint-Lazare. After twenty-two months of detention, in October 1843, she finally appeared before a jury.

She was a woman of medium height whose mild face announced intelligence; her attire, entirely black, was of monastic simplicity. Long dark brown hair, which she wore in falling curls, emphasized her pallor, from which eyes of a great vivacity stood out. She expressed herself very fluently.

On the defense bench, beside the advocate, one of Madame Daren's sons was sitting, a young man of about twenty, a wood-engraver in Paris.

The woman's story testified, at the least, to a very unlucky star. Born in Poland to a very honorable family, she might now have been forty-one years old. A man named Darenne, a professor of France at the College of Warsaw, had asked for her hand and obtained it. Impatient to take advantage of his wife's money, he had departed with her for Paris, where a magnificent position awaited him, he assured her. In fact, he had no resources; his attempts had only ended in poverty. Married in 1819, he had separated from his wife in 1832 and left her with three children to bring up.

"Absolutely nothing remained to me," the accused added at this point. "I did not lose courage I opened a small restaurant and boarding house, first in the Rue Mazarine, then in the Rue Saint-André-des-Arts, and then in the Rue Mignon. My profits averaged ten francs a day. In a few years I amassed savings of three thousand francs, even though I have three dependent children. I was not at the end of my ordeals. In 1839, Romanzoff presented himself at my house with a letter of recommendation. He said that he was a German refugee. I had compassion on the distress that he was then in, and made him numerous advances. That is my only crime. I was absolutely unaware of what Romanzoff did, and I was too discreet to ask him questions on that subject. Later, he assured me that he had received money from his family, and after having hastened to repay me what he owed me, he constrained me, out of jealousy against my compatriots, who ate in my restaurant, to sell my establishment."

The president asked her: "From the Rue Mignon, where did you go?"

"To Passy, to a house rented by Romanzoff, the rent of which he paid."

"Have you not traveled to Prussia with him? What was the objective of that journey?"

"Romanzoff claimed to be a Prussian refugee; his relatives, he said, should be occupied in obtaining mercy for him. He charged me to take a letter and money to one of the members of a family named Herweg, who were to facilitate communication with his own family."

"Where did you find Romanzoff again?"

"He was waiting for me in Liège."

"You had a passport to make that journey. What did you do with it afterwards?"

"Romanzoff asked me for it, for a lady who wanted to go to England. I gave it to him, after having obtaining a visa for that country, and giving him an IOU made out to me by a Pole living in London, whom the lady was to see."

Numerous witnesses were heard. They did not make any denunciation against the woman. Several of them praised her probity.

The prosecutor then spoke, inveighing forcefully against the conduct of the accused, whom he represented as entirely delivered to Romanzoff. "We have the right," he said, "to criticize that conduct highly. This woman has forgotten all the sentiments of honor; she has mistaken her duties as a wife and mother, and no one here can protest against my words."

"I can, Monsieur," shouted a voice departing from the defense bench.

"Who is that man?" asked the president.

"He's the son of the accused," replied the advocate. "Everyone will understand the sentiment that provoked that interruption, and I beg you to be indulgent."

"Have him expelled."

A speech full of details honorable for Madame Darenne, all details perfectly proven, added to the interest that the woman already inspired. She was not only from a very noble Polish family, in whose home the King of Bavaria had not disdained to accept hospitality for a week, but Madame Darenne was also of a character charitable to excess and devout to the point of fanaticism. The following letter, addressed to the defender and signed by one of the lady inspectors of Saint-Lazare, made a deep impression on the audience:

> *Monsieur,*
>
> *I have only learned today the name of Madame Darenne's defender, and I am hastening to acquit a duty toward her by instructing him of facts about which his client has doubtless not spoken to him. Yes, Monsieur, I am sure that Madame Darenne had not said anything to you about the esteem she has been able to conquer here by her mildness, her resignation full of dignity and her boundless devotion for her companions in misfortune. There is not a day of her long detention that has not been marked by some act of kindness and generosity.*
>
> *A few months ago, a nurse brought a little child back to a detainee who owed her*

fifteen francs and could not pay her. The nurse, suspicious and doubtless poor, declared that, having not been paid, she was going to take the child to the foundlings' hospice. The mother was in despair, for the most perverse of our unfortunates still have entrails. The mother implored the poor peasant woman on her knees, who refused—with tears in her eyes, but she refused. Madame Darenne had just received a small sum—very small, since she could not pay the debt in its entirety— but she said with so much emotion: "This is all I have in the world!" and gave her eleven francs, that the nurse declared herself paid and promised to keep the child.

In order to understand how much devotion there is in that action, it is necessary to know the privations to which prisoners without resources are subjected. Madame Darenne has been detained for a long time, and only receives feeble aid from a son whose career has scarcely commenced; and yet, no complaint has ever escaped her. She does not accuse anyone of slowness and injustice! Confident in God, and in her undoubted innocence, she has waited, calm and benevolent, for the day of her deliverance to arrive.

Drawn to her by that all misery inspired in me, I wanted to know whether I was right to accord her more interest than many others. I have obtained information from several

great Polish families and I have discovered
that when refugees from that nation arrive,
before the French government had provided
for their needs, she had given bread to a large
number of her proscribed brethren.[1]

One of the Lady Inspectors
of Saint-Lazare.

Madame Darenne was acquitted.

"My daughter! My daughter!" she cried, falling back on her bench, suffocated by sobs.

X

For many more months, Romanzoff, without ceasing his culpable industry, succeeded in rendering himself ungraspable. His cunning would doubtless not have been sufficient to preserve him from the subtle eye of the agents of the Sûreté; he must have been seconded by a rare good fortune. They were unworried, however, it was highly improbable that a man bold enough to remain in the very milieu where he alarmed so many interests would not fall into the hands of the law some day.

---

1 Poland had been partitioned in 1795 between Russia, Austria and Prussia, and repartitioned again after the defeat of Napoléon in 1815 by a Polish Kingdom that was part of the Russian Empire, the territory of which was gradually annexed by Russia. However, the Poles mounted an active resistance against their conquerors, and fought a long political campaign for independence. An uprising in November 1830 was put down by the Russians, resulting in a flood of Polish refugees in Western Europe, especially Paris.

In fact, a denunciation finally betrayed his incognito. On the fifteenth of September 1846—which is to say, three years later—the forger was arrested at five o'clock in the morning in a house in the Rue d'Anjou Saint-Honoré, where he had been living since the previous tenth of August.

Under the name of Charles René, he occupied at the rear of the courtyard, on the first floor, lodgings that seemed to indicate a lover of the arts. At the sight of the warrant borne by the commissaire de police, the pretended René confessed that he had been born in Rhenish Prussia, and that he had been baptized with the named Theodor Herweg, but that particular circumstances had obliged him to take other names, including that of Romanzoff.

All the equipment of forgery, copper plates and large number of false banknotes, were seized.

The same day, a few moments later, another police commissaire, similarly assisted by the chief of service of the Sûreté, was transported to the Rue de la Tour-d'Auvergne, to the domicile of a language-teacher who adopted the name Antoine Germain. A search led to the seizure of three passports, an imprint of the seal of the Préfecture de Police, a tracing of a banknote, a small iron and copper press equipped with four screws, etc.

No papers bore the name of Germain. The latter declared that his name was Anton von Knapp, that he had been born in Prussia, and that he had been in commerce with Romanzoff for a long time in the crimes committed by the latter,

Herweg and Knapp, both of distinguished appearance, finally appeared at the assizes in September 1847.

Sad to relate, perhaps never had two more intelligent, better-educated and better brought-up young men appeared on the bench of culpables. They did not deny any of the facts laid against them, and gave with a perfect urbanity all the information asked of them.

Knapp's complicity was almost limited to putting the false bills into circulation. His skill was far from being as redoubtable as Romanzoff's. Without the latter it was even certain that Knapp would never have existed. In 1836, he had deserted from the Prussian army, where he was serving as a surgeon's aide, and had taken refuge in Metz. It was in that city that he had met Herweg and entered into liaison with him.

Deprived of a lucrative position, Romanzoff had only just recovered from a grave illness and found himself without resources. He came into the lodgings one morning where Knapp was still in bed, thumped a table with exasperation and cried: "I need three hundred thousand francs, and I shall have them!"

"How?" Knapp said to him.

"I shall make false Prussian treasury bills," replied Herweg.

Knap offered to distribute them, and it was agreed that the proceeds would be divided between them.

Herweg and Knapp had obtained more than forty thousand francs, as many by the emission of false Prussian bills as those of the Société Générale de Belgique.

The debates did not reveal any more salient details regarding Knapp, except that he was a poet. He was, in fact, if one can merit that title by aligning syllables and stitching rhymes therein. To tell the truth, he had given a specimen of his lyric capacities in which it would have been difficult, even with the most partial indulgence, to find anything that might be called a good line.

Letters relating to a duel were seized among Romanzoff's papers, and the latter, interrogated on the subject, replied: "It was a duel I fought with Herr von Knapp, for motives unconnected with the trial, which there is no point in my explaining."

The destiny of Romanzoff, then aged thirty-four, had already been subject to various phases.

"A student at first," he said, "I then entered the Prussian military school. That was in 1830. The fever of liberal ideas had spread throughout Europe. We were given for the thesis of a composition *Military Institutions*. The dissertation I submitted was considered as a work of propaganda. Only my youth saved me from prison. I was expelled from the school.

"Shortly thereafter, the ennui of an unoccupied life made me a bombardier in a Prussian artillery regiment. In 1834, finding myself in Cologne, a man named Balden counseled me—or to put it better, challenged me—to counterfeit Prussian treasury bills. I fabricated a few five-thaler bills. Having been denounced and pursued, I took refuge in Belgium, then in Holland, and then in France.

"For four years I was the director of a factory in Ars, not far from Metz. My salary was eight thousand francs. An argument with one of the foremen in the factory obliged me to renounce that position. It was then that, ill, devoid of resources and desperate, I formed a liaison with von Knapp and resolved to fabricate false Prussian treasury bills. Von Knapp distributed them in Metz, Coblentz and Trèves. His arrest, and his almost immediate escape, had resonance. I judged it appropriate to come and hide in Paris . . ."

His liaison with the woman Darenne was known; it was known that in 1841, with the falsified passport of that woman, he went to England in order to negotiate the false bills of the Société Générale de Belgique. It was in that era that, in a London tavern, he had made the acquaintance of young Pressel, then at grips with great distress. Romanzoff had helped him, and, having recognized his intelligence, had engaged him to come to find him in Paris.

But what had become of him during Madame Darenne's incarceration in Saint-Lazare? That was what his summary integration revealed. He had run away to Italy under the name of Oswald, stayed there for six months and then returned to France. His evil genius had left him no relief. While Madame Darenne was being tried, Romanzoff, retired in a house in the Rue de Sicile, had engraved new plates, fabricated new papers and circulated fake banknotes. The following year, under the name of Linder, he went to Lille, Brussels and Antwerp in order to put them into circulation. That emission had brought him sixty-five thousand francs; von Knapp had not participated in it.

The plate that had been used to print those banknotes had been seized in the Rue d'Anjou Saint-Honoré. They were each for a hundred pounds sterling. Of the forty-nine he had printed, he had only thus far put twenty-seven into circulation. Dated London, the fifth of October 1843, they bore the following subscription in English: *For the Government and the Company of the Bank of England*, and then the signature of one of the cashiers of that bank. Seven different names figured in the various signatures.

He had begun to engrave on a plate the vignettes of a thousand-franc bill of the latest creation of the Banque de France.

"That's true," he said, "but I abandoned that idea. That sketch goes back at least nine months before my arrest."

Sheets of blank paper had also been seized, which presented the same filigree as the Bank of England bills, with the words "Bank of England" raised in two places in the fabric of the paper. An expert chemist testified that all that had been contrived with marvelous artistry.

"The last plate that had served for the fabrication of banknotes," said the graver general of money, "had been made with such intelligence that if I had not received the information from the accused Herweg, I would not have been able to take account of the methods he had employed. It is engraved with a rare exactitude and an extreme perfection. I have procured a genuine banknote from a money-changer, and I admit that it was very difficult to distinguish the fake banknote from the veritable one."

Romanzoff was asked whether it was the paper-factory in Ars that he had learned to fabricate the paper he had used.

"No, Monsieur," he replied. "I taught myself, as soon as I was occupied with that fabrication."

The graver general observed that the accused had given him all the desirable explanations.

"Except for the fabrication of the paper," Romanzoff interjected. "That's my secret."

A juror asked whether it was of any importance to know what method the accused had employed to fabricate the paper.

"A great importance," replied Monsieur Barre. "That secret would be very precious for the Banque de France."

Romanzoff, invited to say whether he wanted to reveal his secret, said: "Willingly, Monsieur, but there would be the greatest danger in divulging it publicly. What presently restricts the number of forgers is the difficulty of fabricating the paper. If I made my secret known publicly, it might be abused."

The emission of 1838 being uncompromised, Herweg had procured with the Prussian thalers eleven thousand francs, with the bills of the Société Générale de Belgique, thirty-five thousand francs, with the ban-knotes, sixty-five thousand francs. Nevertheless, not to mention that Knapp had had his share of the produce of the emission of the Prussian bills and the Belgian bills, the accusation itself observed the Romanzoff had not spent for his personal profit the total of his crimes, that, spontaneously, he had advanced eight thousand francs to a man named Benoît, in whose establishment he took his meals, that he had lent six hundred francs to a Monsieur Juker, in whose house he had resided, and that he had divided various sums in the same manner between persons whom he refused to name.

In the meantime, some interest having been generated by certain details spread regarding Romanzoff, it was agreed that the advocate general, in his speech, was solidly founded in claiming that the two accused were less excusable because they were better endowed and better educated.

He was able to add, without going beyond the bounds of an equitable appreciation;

"These men are more dangerous than highway robbers. One can arm oneself against the latter, while commerce is disarmed against such forgers. In proceeding with the audacity and perseverance that you know them to have, they menace all fortunes. You have only seen one specimen of their redoubtable industry in the emission of bills of all genres, which has procured them a hundred and ten thousand francs . . ."

The condemnation followed. Romanzoff greeted his with the calm resignation of a man who feels justly doomed.

One final detail revealed the cunning ploy thanks to which he had been able to evade research for such a long time. The foreman of the jury, a maire or deputy in one of the surrounding communes, asked whether Herweg admitted being the same person as Romanzoff.

"I have been sent the portrait of the latter," he added, "and that portrait does not resemble in the slightest the man that I have before my eyes."

"In the fugitive's lodgings," the president replied, "A portrait was found that, on certain indications, was wrongly supposed to be that of Romanzoff, which was sent to all the police officers and money-changers in Paris."

Those deceptive indications were the work of Romanzoff's own hand.

Many people, however, were inclined to believe that Theodor Herweg was the martyr of a sort of obsession. The monomania of the forger exists as authentically as that of murder. For years, he had devoted his days and his nights to toil; he had expended more talent, patience, audacity and energy than would have been necessary to assure him of success in a glorious career, only to end inevitably in an abyss that he had glimpsed himself, at intervals, with terror. Had he not been heard to say, twenty times over, in a somber and despairing manner: "Oh, I shall finish badly, I shall finish badly."

At any rate, by virtue of the ensemble of his brilliant qualities, Romanzoff remains, fortunately, a very rare figure. Might it not be the case, furthermore, that the intermittent appearance of such men also has some reason for being? Might it have no other effect, for example, than that of sounding the alarm and warning us that it would be prudent to seek the security of interests elsewhere than in guarantees of a purely material order?

The Man who Nourished Butterflies

I received this note:

> *Near the middle of the Rue des Gravilliers, opposite a copper foundry, in the house of a merchant of paint-brushes, one sees at the door a little display window in a frame, in which a few butterflies are fixed. It is labeled with the name "Pichonnier," followed by: "manufacturer of vegetable-slicers, invites amateurs to climb up to his abode on the second floor, at the back of the courtyard, to see more than three thousand living butterflies, which he has been nourishing for several years."*

With a view to pleasing the person who doubtless flattered himself with piquing my curiosity sharply, I went to that address. But the Rue des Gravilliers is replete with copper foundries and merchants of paint-brushes. The indication given to me was therefore imperfect. I went from shop window to shop window, from foundry to foundry, and I found no trace of any butterfly or Pichonnier.[1]

A few days later, the author of the note affirmed to me verbally that he had seen the aforementioned window-frame, gone up to the second floor, to the apartment of the said Pichonnier, and had seen with his own eyes hundreds of beautiful butterflies in gauze cages.

A breeder of butterflies was, at least, something new. No profound knowledge of natural history is necessary in order to be aware that the insects in question like air, warmth, sunlight and flowers. They appear and disappear. They are not seen, as everyone knows, in winter. Even in summer, when a curtain of clouds intercepts the sunlight, they hide. And yet they could live in a room in the damp Rue des Gravilliers, in the shadow of a cage, like a linnet or a goldfinch! Could it be, in addition, that the passion for living animals descends in humans as far as the frailest insects?

In that preoccupation, I encountered, while visiting the flower-beds of the Jardin des Plantes, a man who attracted my attention. He was a tall old man dressed in a long blue frock-coat. His silk hat, brown with age, was dotted with butterflies, which were fixed there with the aid of black pins. The little creatures were in agony. Holding under his arm, like a book, an oblong box garnished on one face with a mesh of thin iron wire, he was walking alongside the flower-beds without paying

---

1 The surname Pichonnier has existed in France for a long time. It allegedly originated in the Auvergne, where the word was applied to breeders of pigeons.

any heed to curious people. From time to time, I saw him plunge his thumb and index-finger into the calyx of a flower and pull out an object, which he imprinted in his box by means of a little door fitted into it. It was soon evident to me that a multitude of living insects was swarming in that box, for which my man was hunting. I followed him for some time, moved by the idea of having Pichonnier before my eyes. I was about to accost him. The butterflies that were flapping their wings in his hat gave me doubts. A stranger, who observed me observing, made me understand that I was mistaken.

"He's an entomologist," he told me, "who collects insects in order to sell them . . ."

I don't know why, but that mistake, far from extinguishing my desire to see Pichonnier, on the contrary, increased it.

I searched the Rue des Gravilliers from one end to the other. This time my search was successful. Pichonnier had changed domicile. At his former dwelling the concierge gave me a piece of paper with the heading:

Admitted to the Exposition of 1849
(Recompense obtained.) (Honorable mention.)
Rue Vieille-du-Temple
PICHONNIER
Patented Inventor and Manufacturer
s. g. du g.

A list followed of various instruments for slicing vegetables, cutting glass, engraving, piercing, coring apples and pressing cucumbers, after which there was mention of a new method of embalming birds and fish. On the subject of butterflies, however, it remained silent, which led me to think that he might have abandoned that pastime after fruitless trials.

I did not hesitate, however, to go to see him. The practice of industries that had so little in common must, it seemed to me, originate from in a brain in singular confusion. I expected to find a figure who was at least bizarre.

In certain regards, Pichonnier surpassed my expectation. In my memory he was to swell the list of men who, beneath the most ordinary exterior, are like reservoirs of curiosities, and to fortify the opinion, already old in me, that perhaps a man does not exist who does not have his interesting aspect.

On the ground floor, specimens of tools were visible in a small display-window, with a piece of headed paper stuck to the glass. I searched in vain for anything resembling a butterfly. At the name Pichonnier, a woman invited me to go up to the second floor. The door was open.

My gaze fell immediately upon a man of average height, between thirty-five and forty years old, who had nothing notable in his physiognomy except a habitude of suffering and anxious eyes. He was alone, in a small room overlooking a narrow courtyard, having a meager meal on the corner of a table. I was immediately prey to a great sadness. I did not only pay attention to him on penetrating into that silent and bleak room, however; my eyes were drawn in all directions by a collection of strange objects displayed on shelves fitted along the walls and to the ceiling.

"A friend in the provinces," I told him, "who is occupied with natural history, has learned that you breed butterflies. He has charged me to ask you whether you would consent to give him some information on that subject."

I was afraid that he might explode with laughter or anger, but he got to his feet, without showing any surprise.

"Certainly," he said, in a mild and melancholy tone.

That was the entire preamble. He indicated a rather large cage hanging near the window. Gauze was substituted therein for the brass wire of ordinary cages. It was divided into four almost equal compartments. In one of the upper compartments, numerous chrysalides were suspended from the gauze by a wire. In another, to the side, I perceived about twenty living butterflies along the walls of the cage and on the flowers of a reseda and other plants.

"You see here," Pichonnier said to me, "Peacock Butterflies, Painted Ladies, Camberwell Beauties and Glanville Fritillaries. I've had them for a long time. They'll survive the winter."

I thought that I was dreaming. On seeing those little creatures fluttering, imbibing the juice of plants, you would have thought that you were in a garden in the sunlight. As Pichonnier approached they flapped their wings excitedly, the fresh and vivid colors of which they allowed me to admire.

"On the lower level," Pichonnier continued, "there are Tortoiseshells. There are three species: large, small and medium-sized. Each species has its colors. Notice how they nourish themselves, with a little straw. There are fifty of them; they hatched out a week ago. I can keep them alive for as long as I wish."

"That's surprising," I said.

"Here," added Pichonnier, showing me a section in which leaves of mulberry, linden, oak, etc. were scattered pell-mell, "are what I call *drops of blood*, because they have bloodstains on the wings: Nankeens, which are found on oaks, and Silkmoths, or two-eyes. You can see that they do, in fact, have an eye on each wing. It's claimed that they can see with those eyes, but personally, I don't believe it."

To be obliging, I exaggerated my ecstasy slightly.

"Since you're an enthusiast," Pichonnier said to me, "I can show you many other things."

He took me into the next room, in which sunlight entered obliquely, and put me in the presence of a cage divided in two. On one side, innumerable caterpillars were gnawing salad vegetables, making lace of them.

"I've counted them," Pichonnier said to me. "There are four hundred. They're Peacock Butterfly caterpillars. But look over here." He designated the other compartment, where all sorts of butterflies were fluttering. "Here are the Blues, and Green Hairsteaks. You can find the latter at Bondy at this very moment. Look, can you see the Auroras? They come in May, about the twelfth. This yellow one is the Clouded Yellow, that one the Brimstone. Then there's the Swallowtail, the Speckled Wood, and then the Large and Small Fritillaries—the small one hasn't been seen for three years—and the Lithograph! Look at its white wings with black lines."

Some of those names, among others that of the Lithograph, seemed to me to be a trifle adventurous.

"That's quite possible," he replied. "I don't understand any of their baroque names; I baptize them in accordance with my own ideas. That doesn't alter the fact that I know better than anyone their habits, their nourishment and the places where one encounters them. Perhaps I'm the only person who knows where to find the caterpillar of the Red Admiral. I'd be able, in a month's time, to furnish an enthusiast with two thousand magnificent butterflies."

"In your place," I told him, "I'd try."

He shook his head dolorously. "It would be like everything else," he said. "They don't want me to make a living."

"Who are *they*?" I asked,

"How do I know?"

He returned to the first room and showed me a root-trimmer of a very ingenious design. "It's my own invention," he told me. "Only I can make one of those. It's all of a piece; one can't cut one's fingers. Well, they claim that it's worthless because it isn't blessed. They'd like to force me to go to confession. I don't refuse to go, but they leave it to me to marry. I'll go, I'll do as everyone else does. They'll bless my wife, me and my work at the same time . . ."

While I was looking at Pichonnier in amazement, a cicada started to sing, which deflected the fellow's attention.

"Oh, yes," he said, "there are cicadas."

And he took me to the first cage, where I discovered, in one of the lower sections, five or six beautiful cicadas, which, at the sight of Pichonnier, climbed along the gauze as if they knew him.

"They need sunlight, these little beasts," said Pichonnier. "They'd sing differently. I also have crickets."

From a pile of little superposed cages he took one scarcely two inches square. Through a light iron mesh, which allowed daylight to penetrate, I did, in fact, see a cricket in the process of gnawing cake and lettuce. It marked its joy in seeing its master by singing in its turn.

For a moment, in the room, a concert of crickets and cicadas was heard, which might have made one believe that one was in the midst of fields on the evening of a warm day.

Pichonnier enjoyed my astonishment. A few sparks gleamed in his eyes

"I nourish those of all nations," he continued, pointing out to me a bottle on the window sill, in which a tiny frog was sitting on the steps of a ladder, out of the water. It was adorable. As white as milk under the belly, it had a green back, but the very pale green, easy on the eye, of new shoots.

"It's a true tree-frog," said Pichonnier. "It knows me. It comes when I call. *Petite!*"

The frog dived into the water.

"It's going to rain," said Pichonnier, with conviction, without consulting the sky. "The tree-frog is the most reliable barometer that exists."

I looked at the sky. It was all blue. I bit my lip in order not to laugh at the prediction. The hour was not far off when I would remember it.

"Look, look!" said Pichonnier suddenly, with an extreme emotion. His gaze was fixed at that moment on the container of chrysalides. "A Red Admiral is about to hatch! Isn't it beautiful? Because of you, I won't kill it . . ."

He took it delicately in his fingertips and slipped it into the compartment where there were flowers.

The new-born butterfly clung to the gauze, and opened its wings for the first time. Although they were still moist and ragged, it was truly something admirable to see. It was impossible to imagine anything as splendid as the fire-red bands that traversed the velvety black. I could not take my eyes off it.

In the meantime, Pichonnier said: "That's curious. The other day, in the Bois de Vincenes, I saw a naturalist who was running after a Peacock Butterfly. He hurt himself! And why? In order to capture a poor butterfly that was utterly disfigured. I couldn't help laughing internally, thinking that I had hundreds of those butterflies in my room more beautiful than any there have ever been in a showcase of natural history."

I followed the direction indicated by his hand and I saw that there were two large frames on the wall, filled with butterflies, from the largest to the smallest, among the number of which he pointed out the Marbled White, the Silver-Washed Fritillary, the Mill Moth, a small moth that seems to emerge from flour, the Swallowtail, the Giant Peacock Moth, the Oak Eggar, the Horned Moth or Devil Moth, etc., etc.

The intact enamel of their wings had a vivacity of color and a freshness that made one think that they had all hatched yesterday.

"Some die after laying eggs," added Pichonnier. "The others I can keep alive, but I don't keep them because they break their wings."

Many other details were given to me by the worthy man, whose specialist knowledge would have done honor to a professional entomologist.

"You ought to take steps," I said. "Passionate collectors exist, even for butterflies."

"Yes," he said to me, in a melancholy tone. "I would have liked to offer those messieurs a beautiful collection, but I dare not go there. In any case, my enemies would not have suffered it. They've sworn my doom."

Again I considered him with amazement.

"They leave me in poverty," he continued. "They want me to die of hunger. All my relatives are rich. I'm alone. I hired a child to turn my wheel, because one of my legs is almost paralyzed; well, they did so much that he doesn't come any longer. If only they didn't prevent me from marrying."

"Have you never been married?" I asked him.

"They've always opposed it," he replied. "Only recently it was a settled matter. I received a letter recalling me to my homeland for that. I ran to the railway. I arrived...it was to witness the marriage of my wife to someone else. Alas," he said, with increasing melancholy, "it's futile to struggle."

"It's necessary," I said, "not to abandon yourself to discouragement."

"You don't know all that they've made me suffer!" he cried. "Such as you see me, I count thirty-two useful inventions. Here they are, inscribed in this ledger." He showed me a ledger. "I have several patents. Look, here's the root-cutter, the horn-trimmer with several blades, these pastry-wheels, this lemon-press. All that is done to perfection. I also have five models in this drawer, which I'll break one of these days . . ."

I confess that the workmanship of those instruments, very ingeniously conceived, seemed remarkable to me.

"Here's a knife," said Piconnier, taking a knife out of his pocket, "which cuts glass like a diamond."

He did, in fact, cut up several fragments of glass with the tip of the knife. His index finger then made me turn my head toward a large pane of glass on which fantastic human figures were engraved and even more fantastic trees. Various colors had been introduced into the sculptures.

"It's me who engraved all that," he told me. "I've also imagined those large butterflies, more beautiful than nature, to the side. This is one that cost me five francs."

I was finally beginning to get my bearings among the myriads of disparate objects that cluttered the room. On a table, among the utensils invented by Pichonnier, I distinguished a monkey, a parrot, a jay, a chicken with three legs, a squirrel and a drake, all so well-stuffed that one might have thought they were alive.

"I've found a method for embalming birds without any deterioration," Pichonnier told me. "Have you seen anything more frightful than the animals stuffed by naturalists? With the skin of animals that they empty, they make creatures that resemble no known animal. For myself, I don't touch them; I don't empty them; I dry them with the meat. My birds retain their forms. They remain when dead as they were when alive."

"Does your procedure resist time?" I asked.

"Look," said Pichonnier, summoning my gaze to a small item of furniture. "Here's a swift dried by my method ten years ago. I have, however, left it exposed to the air. One would think it had been stuffed today."

He was saying nothing but the truth.

Fish suspended from the ceiling then struck my gaze.

"It's the same for fish," Pichonnier continued. "People cut them from end to end under the belly in order to empty them, and then sew them up. It's frightful. Nothing remains but scales. They have a collection of fish in order to say 'We have one of these.' In fact, their fish are not fish; they're monsters that have never been seen. Look at mine. One would think that they had just emerged from the water. I've devised an implement for emptying them through the gills without touching the scales. With a twist of the wrist, it's done."

Numerous specimens of scales and fins testified, in fact, by their gleam, to his extreme skill.

In sum, my memory was insufficient to contain all the objects that were offered untiringly to my curiosity. Nevertheless, I remember that he opened a cupboard, on the shelves of which a collection of hand-bells fabricated with the aid of wine-glasses was arranged, and he told me that he had found a means of rendering coconut as supple as horn and making knife-hilts from it.

"But what's the point?" he added, ever more somber. "Inventors, while they're alive, are persecuted; it's said that they're madmen and drunkards. Justice is only rendered to them after their death."

I tried to distract him from those funereal thoughts.

"Monsieur," he said, "I ought to be at my ease, but people don't want that. When I go into a shop to sell my instruments, they laugh in my face. Others don't even want to see me, and they throw me out, because they aren't blessed. I've been in the National Guard twenty times. Once, I saved the post. Under Louis Philippe, I should have had a medal. It was someone else who got it in my stead. Even in the house, there's no end to the bad turns done to me. A neighbor came into my apartment recently. He was drunk.

"'Would you like to sell yourself?' he said.

"'I wouldn't find anyone who wanted to buy me,' I replied.

"Then he started turning the tools on my table over and over, disturbing everything, criticizing everything. He told me that my cucumber-press was made on the principle of nutcrackers. I ask you, is it permissible to come into people's homes to molest them thus?

"'Go away,' I said, 'and come back when you're sober. I don't do business with drunkards.'

"Sometimes I find my sign in the middle of the stairs . . . the laundress keeps my linen . . . oh, Monsieur, I'm betrayed by all the nations!"

Physicians will tell you that out of every twenty patients that come to consult them, at least half have imaginary maladies. They don't deny that the latter suffer as much, and sometimes more, than the others. In fact, the miseries of that poor inventor, real or chimerical, had something heart-rending about them.

"It's the same in the provinces," he continued. "I encounter enemies everywhere. In Bayonne, they confiscated more than three hundred francs' worth of merchandise, claiming that I owed eighteen francs. I've never been able to get them back . . ."

It is at least probable that, in the ordinary misfortunes of life, that worthy man saw the gears of a universal conspiracy against his person.

"Dreams are not deceptive, however," he said. "I've noted more than twenty in my ledger. They all have the same meaning. Once there was a huge meadow in the midst of plowed fields, which extended as far as the eye can see. Suddenly, the cats of all nations surged forth into the meadow, white, black, green, red, some with little ears and long tails, others with long ears and short tails. They emerged in thousands from underground. They swarmed like ants in a collapsed ant-hill. In the end, there were so many that the meadow could no longer contain them. Then they invaded the plowed fields. That's quite clear."

"I don't understand," I told him.

"What!" he said. "The cats are treason. The huge meadow is Paris. The plowed fields are the provinces. Paris can no longer hold my enemies, there are so many. They're spreading out into the provinces."

Involuntarily, Pharaoh's dream, interpreted by Joseph, returned to my memory.

"I know very well that I'm bound to succumb," added Pichonnier. "They'll end up murdering me."

"Oh," I said, compassionately.

"I have confidence in God. In any case, to speak frankly, it's better to die than to live like this. If I didn't have these little beasts . . ."

He paraded his gaze and his hand around the room.

At that moment, as if to respond to him and console him, the cicadas and the crickets started singing again, definitely started to sing.

A sentiment of profound sadness oppressed me. The time to withdraw had come. My visit had distracted the poor man somewhat. He engaged me to come back, on the pretext of seeing the Red Admiral whose hatching I had witnessed. I promised him that, and quit him.

Scarcely was I outside than rain fell in torrents. How could I not recall the tree-frog's prediction? For not having believed it, I was soaked to the skin.

Irma Gilquin

I

JOHN MAXWELL descended from a rich and honorable Edinburgh family. All that was known about him was what he said himself—which is to say, only a few details. In the universities in which he had sojourned by turns until the age of twenty, Maxwell sometimes took vanity from the fact that his mind had found studies incessantly repugnant, even those that demanded the least application. Apart from equitation, fencing, boxing, swimming, hunting and races, nothing interested him.

Robust in constitution, his head empty of ambition, his soul in his flesh, not only had he not escaped the despotism of any appetite, he had never even been worried by the need to struggle against that slavery. Under the exclusive empire of that vocation of pleasure, two or three years at the most after his majority, he had already devoured half of a considerable patrimony.

It was then that, banished by his family, confused himself by his celebrity in the bad places of London, and pursued by the vague desire to secure his independence by saving what remained of his fortune, he had resolved to settle in France.

His instinct had served him well; merely by the fact of that emigration he found himself richer than he had been in his homeland at the outset. In Sologne, above all, a land of legendary poverty, in a château buried in the middle of woods, where horses, dogs and hunting were no longer a source of ruination for him, his income was more than sufficient, and beyond his appetites, his passions, his liberality and, better still, his incurable insouciance in matters of material interest.

There, as elsewhere, the choice of his liaisons reposed uniquely on hazard. The quality of people mattered little to him, provided that he had joyful and noisy companions. His château was never empty of parasites that he recruited in the town, and with whom, to say everything summarily, he hunted, rode, fenced, played billiards or cards, and spent his nights drinking.

The privilege of stopping him on that slope fell to a woman. Although the rumor occasioned by his marriage soon died down, the adventure served nevertheless to inspire fabulous commentaries for a long time. Judge, however, how scantly romantic the story was.

Maxwell went to town every day. Always going to the same inn, he naturally followed the same route to arrive there. The prospect of a new adventure suddenly prompted him to deviate from his habitual route.

Clad in a long white frock-coat, with a red cravat, it was difficult, in the narrow and tortuous streets that he now traversed, to escape attention, especially perched as he was on top of a hunting carriage harnessed to two magnificent horses, which he guided himself, with an idle groom at his side. His affectation in spurring his horses and making them whinny in front of the stall of a poor butcher, at whose counter the charms shone of a tall and fresh young woman, quickly betrayed the secret of his new itinerary.

A conversation at table had given birth in Maxwell to the desire to see that young woman. The enthusiasm with which his friends had talked about her appeared to have warmed him up; scarcely had he seen her than he caught fire, all the more readily because, in his thought, even the grimmest virtue, reduced to such an obscure condition, could not hold out for long against the lure of a gold mine.

Details collected here and there fortified his illusion further. Irma Gilquin was the oldest of the children of a worthy man whom the demands of his excessively numerous family condemned to a perpetual poverty. Barring a miracle, the dazzling beauty of the young woman was bound to fade away in the shadow of a counter to which she was attached by the implacable rigidity of a mother who was consecrated herself to difficult household duties.

John was, therefore, well-founded in thinking the seduction facile. He was, however, mistaken. Without giving evidence of either anger or scorn, Irma sent away coldly the old woman charged with the initial overtures. To increasingly pressing attempts, supported by the glamour of a considerable present, the young woman responded that she would not fail in her duty for a million and that she would only belong to her husband.

Every woman, in sum, is worthy of self-esteem.

Under the empire of an amour multiplied tenfold by resistance, Maxwell implored the young woman at least to consent to a meeting. The go-between offered her house and the guarantee of her honorable assistance. Irma, whose character put her above dread and opinion, granted a rendezvous.

That rendezvous threatened to have no result. The young woman remained as insensible to the most urgent protestations of attachment as to the prestige of a fortune, and persisted with intrepidity in the resolution only to belong to the man whose wife she would be.

At the last moment, however, Maxwell, in an irresistible surge of passion, promised resolutely, on his honor, to marry the young woman very imminently. The unique condition of that, an express condition, was an abduction previous to the marriage. Irma agreed, doubtless estimating that with an honest man, a promise was worth a contract, and perhaps also trusting in her beauty and her courage. The next day she deserted the paternal home in order to go with John Maxwell to his Château des Ormes.

Before then she had left a few words in her bedroom addressed to her father and mother:

My dear parents, until further notice maintain silence regarding my disappearance and have no anxieties on my subject. I am departing of my own will with a man

who has sworn an oath to give me his name.
You will see me three months from now
worthy of you—which is to say, married to
an honest man—or you will never see me
again. Believe in the unalterable respect of a
daughter who loves you tenderly.

Irma Gilquin.

That abduction, however, no matter what the family did, caused some rumor. Irma's return caused even more. With no other dowry than her virtue, which she exposed somewhat to adventure on the faith of one of those promises of which mores authorize, in a sense, the falsification, she came back, against all expectation, legitimately married to a millionaire, bringing her family joy and ease.

Such an astonishing fortune could not fail to awaken envy, or at least to provoke astonishment. For a fortnight there was no talk of anything else in the town.

Far from appearing in the least ashamed of having been reduced to that marriage, however, Maxwell heaped his wife ostentatiously with cares and attentions. His amour seemed to have grown with possession; it was a veritable bewitchment. Irma held him, so to speak, enchained at her knees, to the point that one could believe momentarily that she had fixed him there. Under the influence of that seemingly very gentle servitude, he had renounced liaisons of hazard for nearly two years, in order to lead an exemplary life, and had taken conjugal complaisance so far as to abstain from getting drunk, as he had previously done periodically.

But that species of heroism gradually cost him too much effort not to reach its end soon. Already at grips with an increasing ennui, he had returned to his old and dear habits many a time. At first, Irma had been unable to resolve to close her eyes to those aberrations. Painful struggles had followed; incessant quarrels had troubled the peace of the household, until the day when the young woman, war weary or finally having become clear-sighted, resolved not to argue with her husband any longer, or, so to speak, to put a bridle around his neck.

From that moment on, John gradually resumed integrally his bachelor life. Today, as in the past, when he went to town, he brought back new comrades, whom he fed for entire months, and with whom he spent his money and his life. A man all instinct and caprice, it chanced that once, in his adventures, he gave evidence of some constancy. His unlucky star had put him in conjunction—the word is apt—with a painter in passage whose mediocrity, under the name of Claude Saint-Martin, enjoyed a vogue of sorts in the bourgeoisie of the town. Seduced at first by the painter's proud stature, swashbuckling airs and verve of a traveling salesman, Maxwell, from their second meeting, was possessed by even more enthusiasm, and during the third, only recovered the calm of his senses after having convinced his new friend to come and spend a week or two at the Château des Ormes.

The painter's sojourn there was gradually prolonged to more than six months. His departure, to tell the truth, definitely took on a strange character of necessity; no amiable invitation any longer raised any obstacle to it—far from it. After having been the pampered, fêted and caressed guest of the château thus far, he suddenly found himself shamefully expelled by the implacable hatred of Irma and the insulting indifference of Maxwell.

II

The Château des Ormes is nothing but a vast and old two-story house in gray stone, roofed with tiles, with stables, a kennel and a fine kitchen garden. It is situated two or three hours walk from the town of La Ferté in Sologne. On the ground floor, a glazed door, opening at an equal distance from the two corners of the façade, gives access to a vestibule that traverses the house all the way through and permits a glimpse of the verdure of the trees beyond. From the foot of the façade, the eye embraces a sandy semicircular courtyard, which designs a dense enclosure of bushes, shaded by a magnificent beech more than a hundred years old which rises in the center, in the axis of which extends a long avenue of poplars, closed at the point of its junction with the départmental road by a heavy iron grille.

That sandy courtyard, the bushes that frame it, the few baskets of geraniums and vervain that blossom here and there, the boxed orange trees, oleanders and pomegranates arranged to the right and left of the entrance door, give the initial impression of a well-maintained property. It is sufficient to stroll around the house to form an entirely contrary idea. On the other side, the grass grows all the way to the foot of the walls. On the terrain, which lowers gradually and forms an extensive and profound valley that is dominated by the house, disorderly bushy woodland has gradually disrupted the economy of a beautiful park that once prospered here. All trace of the human hand has disappeared. Weeds have invaded the paths, which, worn away by rain, are mostly impracticable. In the surrounding area, for a league around, there is no roof visible; it is solitude.

It had rained all day; as evening approached, although the rain had stopped, a thick mist still veiled the sky and hastened the night. It was the beginning of autumn; the wind was blowing from the west, and with a noise comparable to that of a downpour on sand, shook off the water with which the branches were soaked. A domestic in a red smock had closed the shutters, the blinds and the doors of the house. Inside, everything was in repose, except in one room on the first floor, where a scene was unfolding apparently unworthy of holding the attention, but which was nevertheless to determine a moving and terrible catastrophe.

Two men were there, one thirty years old at the most, the other at least thirty-five, sitting not far from a fire of vine-stocks.

Maxwell, the younger, blond, beardless, with somewhat pointed features and blue eyes illuminated by drunkenness, was facing his friend Saint-Martin, a powerful man whose long hair and beard recalled the type of certain veterans of the studio.

An uncleared table, on which glasses and bottles were scattered, separated them.

It was a farewell banquet. Maxwell was taking the painter back to the town the following day. One last debauch preceded the hour of separation.

Both were speaking at the same time. Metaphysics, art and morality served as themes for their lively controversies.

Wine has the well-known virtue of inciting grave discussions in people who, when sober, gladly abstain from similar discussions.

They forgot themselves to the extent that a maidservant, who entered without precautions, had to advance very close to the table in order to be noticed by them.

"Monsieur John!" she cried.

Maxwell turned his head swiftly.

"Madame has sent me to beg you," the young peasant girl continued, "not to leave tomorrow before having seen her. She has commissions to give you for her mother,"

John, whose face had cleared as if by enchantment, responded affirmatively by voice and gesture. "Hey, Justine," he added, immediately, "you seem to be in a hurry."

The young woman was, in fact, in haste to go. "Madame is waiting for me," she replied.

With a bound, Maxwell launched himself slyly toward the door, and closed the passage with his tall stature. "I just have a few words to say to you," he said.

Justine recoiled without paying any heed to the painter. She had a seductive freshness and prettiness; her dark eyes, her cheeks, her lips and her chin all smiled in her physiognomy. Maxwell was looking at her with an ardent eye; he seemed possessed by the demon of lust.

"You're charming!" he exclaimed, suddenly.

"In truth," replied Justine "you won't have the first use of it."

"I'm mad about you!"

"You are for all women, except your own."

Full of liveliness and seemingly very tranquil, the young woman nevertheless maintained the same distance between herself and her master. He attempted to approach her, but she immediately drew away to the same extent.

"Listen," he said then, "be reasonable, and no later than tomorrow I'll bring you a beautiful pair of earrings from the town."

"How you go on!" said Justine, laughing. "Another would at least be restrained before society."

The allusion evidently concerned Saint-Martin, who, sunk in his armchair, was smoking his pipe without saying a word and affecting the most profound disdain for what was happening around him.

"You're joking," said John. "What interest would Saint-Martin have in committing an indiscretion?"

The painter shrugged his shoulders disdainfully and indicated by the expression how long the scene seemed to him.

"To the earrings," Maxwell added, "I'll add a gold chain to put around your neck."

Justine became serious. "For your weight in gold," she said, "I wouldn't consent to be scorned. And your wife, in any case, is so good to me! I wouldn't dare look her in the face. She'd kill me with a gaze. Let me tell you once and for all, then, that your pretentions are only tormenting me uselessly."

John took no account of the warning; he pursued the young woman and tried to seize her.

"I'll scream!" said Justine, resolutely, who put the table between them with a bound.

The young man stopped. "So be it," he said, withdrawing from her passage, "but I hope you'll change your opinion."

"You'd be wrong to count on it."

So saying, Justine leapt forward and escaped, pulling the door shut behind her.

In the fireplace, all flames a little while ago, nothing any longer remained but red embers. The light was reduced to the pale rays of a candelabrum with two candles, astray on the table among the bottles and glasses. Apart from the space measured by the table and those sitting at it, the chamber was plunged in an obscurity near to darkness. That, however, was of little concern to the two friends, who had already resumed drinking and arguing. Justine had only interrupted a quarrel about the stars to ignite one about women. Her virtue or stubbornness suggested an observation to the artist that engaged the contest gently.

"Decidedly, my poor John," he said, between two jets of smoke, "you'll never be anything but a child with women."

"Why?"

"You have fifty or sixty thousand francs a year to eat," Claude replied, "you're young, tall, well-made and robust, and you resign yourselves, with such advantages, to the refusal of a maidservant, and let her make a fool of you."

"What means is there of doing otherwise?" said John, sullenly.

"First of all," the artist continued, "not offering an inconsequential girl a price that gives her an exaggerated notion of her value. It's not customary to exalt things for which one's haggling. You act like a worthy son of Albion, royally, but without reflecting that these foolish auctions spoil the child and render her intractable."

If it was evident that the role of pedagogue pleased the painter, it was no less the case that Maxwell, at that moment, seemed disinclined to that of schoolboy.

"And?" he said, drily.

"And," Claude retorted, "it's always a great mistake to appear to be putting in doubt the surrender of the fortress one is besieging."

"To speak clearly," said John, in a voice pierced with irony, "what would you do if you were in my place?"

"Pooh," said Saint-Martin, whose face expanded with conceit, "I'll only tell you that if I only deigned to want . . ."

"Oh, leave me alone," said Maxwell, brutally. "You're nothing but a braggart and a blusterer."

Even in his fits of anger, John had never said anything sharper. In his mouth, that violent remark had all the characteristics of the most revolting insult. A few details regarding the artist and the intimacy of his relations with Maxwell will make that understandable.

III

Among all the arts, only that of miniaturist had smiled on Saint-Martin's ambition. If necessary, he did not disdain to paint life-size portraits, and would not have hesitated to cover twenty feet of canvas or even thirty, but he always returned passionately to painting with a magnifying glass for lockets, brooches and the bezels of rings. Superficial notions on all things, notions collected at the hazard of encounters, made him the most intrepid contradictor in the world. After drinking, talking theology or metaphysics seemed *de rigeur* to him; in his hours of sobriety, to speak frankly, he dealt with less serious questions. The studio argot with which he enameled his language, his obscene equivocations, his repertoire of lewd stories, his ostentatious impiety, and, on top of that, his love of mocking everything to excess, completed giving him the value of an exemplary figure.

In the eyes of anyone who consented to believe him, especially in his profession, he had no rival. As certain people said of Rubens, people said "the palette" of Claude Saint-Martin. But for his horror of back coats and intrigues, he would already have had the red ribbon for years and would be in the Institut.

The success and fortune of less audacious charlatans have been seen all too frequently.

If it were a matter of architecture, sculpture, music or poetry, no artist, even the most surprising, was capable of reasoning better than him. As regards chemistry, astronomy, medicine, the military art, history, voyages etc., the greatest schools and the greatest captains could have profited from his perceptions.

Knowing from a reliable source the very special aversion of Maxwell for numbers, he traced on the wall one day in charcoal a series of algebraic signs, and tried to oblige his friend to attempt to find a resolution to the problem. John protested his ignorance as one defends oneself from a crime.

"You'll never be anything but a donkey!" Saint-Martin then cried, triumphantly. Then, heaping letters on letters, signs on signs and equations on equations, he fell into an armchair, exhausted, and added: "Do you understand . . . ? No . . . ? However, it's as facile as swallowing a glass of water."

In his fury to surpass, he took a curé to task on the catechism in the vicinity of the cathedral, and by dint of shouting, reduced the old incumbent to silence.

With farmers, millers, masons and workers of all states, his inexhaustible loquacity worked marvels. He dazzled them by means of the abuse of technical terms with which his memory was crammed, and wagged his tongue so much that he sometimes succeeded in convincing them that he really was of the métier.

Of a height almost equal to John's, but massive in the shoulders and with the plumpness that precedes obesity, he had the troubled gaze, lax features and livid complexion of a man whose life has been full of inconsiderate libertinage. His long chestnut-brown hair, pretentiously thrown back, only discovered a narrow and receding brow. A thick red beard dissimulated an empty mouth and an excessively short chin, without succeeding in enhancing a mask in which cynicism burst forth with no less force than vanity. The deliberate disorder of his costume would, in any case, have been sufficient to betray him. By his carelessness of chic, one recognized very quickly one of those men who embrace what is called "a career in the arts" less to distinguish himself from the vulgar by meritorious works than by a singular appearance.

His vanity did not even suffer that physical imperfections should be natural disgraces in him. Thus, the inclination to the left of the tip of his humped and broken nose was, he affirmed, only the result of an accident. He was not yet ten years old; a juggler, putting a coin on his nose in order to remove it with a whip, had only succeeded at the cost of flattening the nose against the cheek. It was the same for his legs, slightly bowed like the branches of a measuring compass; it was the fault of his parents, who had made him acquire the habit of riding a horse too soon. Meanwhile, although he boasted of holding himself in a saddle better than a Hungarian, John had never been able to persuade him to mount even the gentlest horses in his stable.

After that, it would have been at least extraordinary if he did not have a skill at fencing to drive all present and future masters of arms to despair. Unfortunately, he had sworn an oath before a tribunal to which he had been summoned in the wake of a due never to touch a sword again as long as he lived.

On the other hand, at billiards and cards, John always found in him a complaisant and indefatigable partner.

With regard to men of that sort, moderate sentiments seem impossible; it is certain that they always
inspire either ardent sympathies or a profound repul-
sion. At the same time as inconstancy drew Maxwell to
such liaisons, the want of intellectual exercise explained
his infatuation with that kind of braggart. Because he
had hardly lived until that day with anyone but grooms
and horse-traders, everything was new for him. In
the beginning, particularly, his enthusiasm tended to
fanaticism. Claude, with his apparently inexhaustible
baggage of anecdotes, cock-and-bull stories, charges
and obscenities amused him, charmed him and impas-
sioned him. He accepted the painter's assertions as so
many verses of the Gospel, mistook for pure gold the
scrap metal of his encyclopedic knowledge, allowed his
boasting to impose upon him, and ended up believing
him to be an entirely superior man. So, not content to
appear glorious to such a guest, to listen to him open-
mouthed with the expression with which a mastiff
impeded by fat watches a greyhound bounding and
running, he suffered that the artist treated him like a
schoolboy and rebuked him, making him ashamed of
his ignorance, and sometimes heaped him with mockery whose coarseness bordered on insult.

That was nothing.

In imitation of enthusiasts, Maxwell spread propaganda, and set out to make others share his admiration.

Irma, who had made it an inflexible rule never
to socialize with the guests of the château, whoever
they were, had intended at first to subject the painter
to that exclusion. On that matter, her husband had

persecuted—or, to put it better, tyrannized—her until, out of lassitude, she had consented to see Saint-Martin. Already edified as to the humor of the wife, the latter had shown himself as modest and reserved toward her as he was the opposite with John. He had promptly acquired the secret of their antagonism, and, having no need to worry about the sentiments of the husband, he had applied himself without respite to conciliate the good graces of the wife.

A vulgar comedy had sufficed for that result. Irma, involuntarily, had gradually been gained by the incessant flattery of her beauty, her judgment and her merits. In whatever matter, she was always right, John always wrong. Claude never wearied of admiring her and feeling sorry for her. Thanks to that tactic, all the passionate prejudices of the husband had slid insensibly into Irma's heart; she and the artist had ended up getting along so well that Maxwell, jealous not of his wife but of the painter, at grips with a violent chagrin, had begun to sulk ridiculously, like a child, and to spend every day outside, hunting or riding, on horseback or in a carriage in the surrounding area. His faith in Irma's beauty was so entire that it had not come to his mind once to suspect the honesty of the relations, more intimate every day, that she had with Saint-Martin.

However, further incidents having occurred, that state of things had ceased abruptly. After having neglected his friend for more than two months, Claude had suddenly drawn nearer to him. In many respects he seemed changed. Thus, the cigarettes that he had smoked until then were replaced by a long wooden pipe, which he took out of his bag to solder it to his lips. To the scorn of his pretended sobriety and his tirades against incontinence, he suddenly had a gluttonous appetite and absorbed such quantities of liquid that John found in him, if not a master, at least a redoubtable rival. At the same time, before Irma, he removed his mask of reserve and forgot himself to the extent of risking obscene jokes.

At that metamorphosis, Irma had at first only been confused; she was soon at grips with a muted anger. Her relations with the artist, so slow to be knotted, had been broken in the blink of an eye, and broken unsparingly on Irma's part. She was not content to refuse absolutely to see him again; she only mentioned him in a hateful tone full of disgust. If he found himself fortuitously in her presence, he had to submit to her arrogant manner and her scornful silence. She did not even hesitate to say to her husband one day, loudly enough to be heard by Claude: "Are you not soon going to spare me the torture of encountering that man?"

Maxwell, very glad to have recovered his friend, had not even thought of trying to find the key to the enigma; he had only wanted to see, in that sudden aversion, a further proof of the inconstancy of the character of women. Nevertheless, John had only escaped imperfectly from the influence that his wife had once exercised upon him. In spite of himself, she still imposed on him. Hence, it was not possible that his prejudice in favor of a man for whom Irma showed so much repugnance could be maintained for long with the same energy. Without him suspecting it, his wife's disdain removed from the painter his surest prestige.

After four or five months at the château, the artist had exhausted his repertoire, and was reduced to issuing a second edition of his puns, his jokes, his aphorisms and his boasts. In brief, he was repeating himself, and Maxwell did not take long to perceive it. From day to day his prodigious consideration for the painter was necessarily diminished.

Like enthusiasm, disenchantment is subject to the law of the inclined plane, and does not suffer any pause. In any case, as John opened his eyes to the light, the memory of the mortifications he had had to suffer returned to his mind. Internally, the idea of breaking his idol and tipping him from a usurped pedestal smiled at his rancor. He had come to remain insensible to the painter's most exorbitant buffooneries, to stand up to him, and even to give him unequivocal signs of impatience.

Add that Claude, exasperated by so many disappointments, had only committed blunders in trying to reconquer the lost terrain. He had been forced to understand that his reign was over, and that his position was becoming less tenable every day, and that it was time to flee if he wanted to escape the insults with which inconvenient parasites are unfailingly showered.

It was eventually agreed: the next day, at daybreak, Maxwell was to take Claude back to the town. But that departure, settled under the pressure of a moral constraint, ignited a resentment in the painter that he had difficulty dissimulating. Impotent, in addition, to pardon the scorn of the wife and the cooling of the husband, he seemed only to be waiting for a pretext to exercise against them reprisals worthy of memory.

In his ears, an item of abuse had just resounded that brought to a peak the outrages of which he believed he had to complain. In fact, among all the things in regard to which his vanity fermented, there was one chapter above all—that of women—in which that vanity, put in vibration, overexcited him to the point of dementia. There was no limit to his fury, therefore, when John, whom he had never wanted, and did not want, to see as anything but a great child of rickety intellect, emancipated himself to the point of daring to say to his face, with regard to gallantry: "You're nothing but a braggart and a blusterer."

IV

Claude shuddered as if he had been struck in the face. Under the action of the wound inflicted on his self-esteem, the ridiculous epithet with which the husband of an adulterous woman is pursued rose to his lips. The whim was all the more surprising because he could not speak without denouncing himself. However, he only recoiled with effort before the enormity of the treason. His constrained mutism was reminiscent of the anguish of a man defending himself against the vertigo caused by the depth of an abyss. He looked at John with eyes in which bitterness and hatred shone; he resembled a dog ready to pounce on a prey.

However, the glimmers of reason that still occasionally traversed his mind, already somewhat troubled by drunkenness, induced him, if not to abandon, at least to defer the confession of a secret whose divulgence, it seemed, ought to be adequate to his vengeance.

After a long pause, he suddenly shook himself and seized his glass.

"Let's drink!" he said in a detached tone.

At the same time as he had got carried away, Maxwell had abruptly pivoted on his axis; he no longer presented to the painter anything but the sinuousities of a profile contracted by ill humor. The amicable provocation of the artist turned him to stone.

"What!" the latter added, putting his glass down noisily on the table. "I pardon, because of your youth, a gibe as insulting as it is ill-timed, and that's your gratitude? Know, then, that it would be sufficient for me to open my mouth to drive back down your throat the unfortunate remark that has just emerged from it."

John raised his head again and looked at the painter with a challenging expression.

"Pure talk, that," he said, shrugging his shoulders.

The features of the irascible Saint-Martin betrayed once again the sentiments of hatred and wrath to which he was prey.

"Oh, my dear," he said, in the midst of a sudden extinction of the voice, "on what grass are you walking? Would you like to avenge on me your insufficiency with regard to women? It would be more befitting, it seems to me, since it finally pleases you to play the man, to utilize the first fruits of your courage to shake off the yoke of the skirt."

208

In response to that sarcasm, Maxwell claimed haughtily that he was not subject to anyone's yoke.

The story of his marriage to a woman to whom, by his own admission, he had flattered himself that he would never give any other title than that of mistress, did not awaken any confusion in him.

To Claude, who evoked that memory, he replied: "I had sworn an oath to marry her."

All the cynicism lurking in the depths of the artist's heart rose to the surface.

"Damn!" he said. "How you go on. Only half of my oaths, if I had been feeble enough to keep them, would have reduced me a seraglio more numerous than the Grand Turk's."

John responded in the most phlegmatic manner: "That would be to recommence what I have done before."

"Pooh," said Claude. "A woman who does not hesitate to refuse you the door to her bedroom."

"Undoubtedly, when I'm drunk; that's her right. It would be odious to do violence to her on the subject of a habit for which she has a horror. Apart from that, I hold her to be an attentive, devoted wife of an unalterable equality of humor."

"Of course!" retorted the artist, mechanically, in whose ears the praise of Irma resonated badly. "From the moment you give her a liberty equal to yours, in what regard would her ill humor burst forth?"

At that strange observation, Maxwell straightened up and looked his adversary in the eyes.

With the assurance of conceit on his forehead and a malign smile on his lips, the painter endured that gaze without understanding with what he was threatened. He was impotent to modify his opinion of his friend, in whom he was obstinate in seeing only an inoffensive young man with whom one could take all possible license without danger. Nevertheless, from that moment on, John only had a borrowed calm.

"That's true," he said, with the air of a man yielding to good reasons—"although," he added nonchalantly, "it does not appear that she is thinking of taking advantage of that liberty."

Saint-Martin immediately retorted: "It appears quite simply that with regard to women you do not share the opinion of the famous Jehan de Meung."[1]

Maxwell admitted that he did not understand, and Claude, in a voice embarrassed by drunkenness, hastened to cite the infamous lines to which he had just made allusion.

"You do indeed see me disposed to sustain," John replied, still apparently calm, "that that assertion, with regard to Irma, is a calumny. I would pledge my hand against proof of the contrary."

---

1 Jehan de Meung who lived in the late thirteenth century, continued and concluded the *Roman de la Rose* begun by Guillaume de Lorris, the best-known, most popular and most controversial of all allegorical Medieval romances. Whereas the first author had set out firmly within the tradition of courtly romance, respectful of the ideals of chivalry and courtesy, Jehan de Meng satirized those ideals mercilessly and misogynistically, criticizing the alleged perfidy of woman and offering strategic advice to seducers desirous of overcoming their defensive wiles.

"Be careful of such a pledge," cried the artist, sniggering, "unless you intend to become one-armed . . . !"

Suspicion slid into Maxwell's heart; he was livid with anger. In the very violence to arrive at certainty he drew on the resources of a comedy for which, by his nature, he had no aptitude. His trembling hand embraced, doubtless unintentionally, the neck of a bottle that contained something other than wine. The glasses, filled to the brim with alcohol, were emptied in the blink of an eye by the two adversaries.

"Is it, by chance," said John, with sweat on his brow and haggard eyes, striving to smile, "that my wife has had, to your knowledge, some weakness that authorizes you to speak as you are doing?"

"Ha ha," said Saint-Martin, with a further snigger.

"Come on, confess it," added Maxwell. "Jealousy, as you know, is the least of my faults. I don't have the right, in any case, to be jealous; that's agreed. Irma is free; it isn't to be feared that I would ever constrain her penchants."

"And that's very wise," said Claude, impudently, "for it's probable that you'd lose your Latin in that."

To see John vacillating on his seat, it seemed that a snake was biting his entrails; apart from that, his eyes were wandering randomly and his fingers were caressing the relief of objects within his reach.

It was a state that had never been attained by the most energetic expression of that man, who, even amid the invasions of drunkenness, impotent to repel a horrible idea, harassed by devouring anguish, was still trying, in order to deceive his enemy, to appear tranquil, and even to smile.

His energy could not be sufficient to sustain such a role for long, and his patience finally failed him.

Fatigued by playing the diplomat, at a pure loss, he suddenly said to the painter, fixing his ardent eyes upon him: "Listen; I hold the story of your amours in general to be a tissue of impostures, and that's why I called you a braggart and a blusterer. That's not enough; founded in believing that your present insinuations repose on nothing serious, I want, unless you proceed with categorical assertions, to join with those epithets those of a knave, calumniator and coward!"

Maxwell was speaking in a muted voice, more embarrassed by rage than drunkenness. His eyes were bloodshot and his lips white with foam. The ferocious instincts of a boxer seemed to have awakened within him.

His adversary, unfortunately, had a brain no less troubled. He was, in addition, tormented remorselessly by the memory of the affronts that were expelling him from the château. The rancor accumulated within him and the thirst for vengeance took him by the throat and strangled him. Those last insults, twisting to breaking point his unique sensitive string—which is to say, his self-esteem—finished by giving him vertigo.

It was said of a man that he had a vanity so great that it would even be capable of inspiring him to a great action. Saint Martin, by contrast, did not recoil before an infamy.

"You're also too naïve," he said, in a half-mocking and half-furious fashion, "to believe that, in my three months of intimacy with your wife, I've only been pre-occupied with her portrait."

The remark was not finished when John, forcing himself to stand up, seized a bottle and menaced the painter with it. The latter, without wasting a second, followed that example exactly. The two projectiles departed at the same time. Instead of going past one another and reaching their intended targets, they met half way and shattered into a thousand pieces. Shards of glass inundated the table, the armchairs and the room.

Meanwhile, the two champions, marching toward one another, unsteadily, seized one another by the collar, the body, the throat and the hair, and rolled on the floor together amid the fragments of the bottles. Not content to stammer oaths and utter savage cries, they used fists, fingernails and teeth against one another furiously.

Such a battle has nothing essentially picturesque. It is even appropriate to draw a veil over it as soon as possible. The prelude to a terrible drama, it was in any case devoid of immediate danger for two men who could not even recall its duration. Their attempts only ended in using up the strength that drunkenness had left them. In the midst of the struggle, their muscles relaxed, their vision was troubled, memory was extinguished within them, and incoherent words fluttered on their lips; they soon plunged into ecstasy, and from ecstasy, they did not take long to slide into a profound slumber . . .

V

The darkness, meanwhile, was succeeded by the dawn and daylight, but a daylight almost as pale as a twilight. A rainy atmosphere the color of lead intercepted the fires of the rising sun. Irma had already quit her bed. Enveloped in a floral cashmere peignoir, shod in furry slippers, head and neck bare, she drew her curtains and opened one of her windows. That window, on the first floor of the façade opposed to that of the courtyard, overlooked the entire valley on the ridge of which the house was built. As far as the eye could see, the gaze floated over masses of verdure, undulating at the caprice of the slope and the folds of the terrain, already magnificently colored by all the autumnal hues.

Under the humid sky, from the bosom of that ocean with waves that were by turns green, pale brown, bloody, yellow and the color of rust, rose the discreet voices of innumerable birds, as if in prayer, the chirping of which, by the very fact of an immense variety, produced a confused, singular, inexpressible, enchanting harmony.

In truth, those mysterious perspectives did not speak to Irma's eyes; those intoxicating sounds had no meaning for her heart; leaning nonchalantly on the sill, she gazed without seeing, and listened without hearing; she simply seemed eager to breathe a fresher air than that of her bedroom.

It would have required a great deal, however, for her appearances to be those of a vulgar nature. Apart from the fact that she was tall for a woman, that the breadth of her shoulders announced that she was becoming powerful, that the proportions and elegance of her upper body, her limbs, her feet and her hands would have tempted the art of a master, all those details only stood out, in a way, in order to concur, with a marvelous ensemble, with the intensity of a physiognomy full of interest and charm. Her neck, although bronzed by the sun, was splendid, and bore the head with infinite grace. A blurred crown of chestnut-colored hair, thick and shiny, sketched the arch of the forehead, for which thin eyebrows comparable to twin strokes of a pen, served as foundations. While the nose, the mouth, the chin and the oval of the face, whose whiteness was tinted in the cheeks by beautiful roseate hues, emphasized by their firm contours a character of the most energetic temper, capable of the most extreme resolutions, the ardors contained in an expansive soul and the anxiety of unsatisfied needs ignited in her brown eyes a veritable conflagration, the reflections of which illuminated the whole face. On top of that, she walked admirably well; the measured movement of her stride imprinted on her curved and supple figure, throughout her body, oscillations of an irresistible seduction.

In the Château des Ormes, where fortune had buried her, her beauty only existed for the mirror; the force of which her soul was the hearth turned to her torture. Maxwell did not love her with an amour exclusive enough to sacrifice his passions to it. Constrained, after an accord of eighteen months, to keep him at a distance, and also to renounce the joys of maternity, she saw disappearing from her horizon the consoling perspectives that the marriage had opened to her, and was gradually gripped again by the species of lethargy in which she had languished at the paternal counter.

In the midst of the racket of guests who filled and emptied the château incessantly, her solitude was profound. Of the few resources at her disposal to break the uniformity of the days, the majority only had in her eyes the charm lent to an insipid life by the most insignificant distractions. It was thus that she came to mount a horse or take aim at birds around the house, to play billiards with Justine, or to exercise in her bedroom snuffing out candles with pistol shots. The last exercise pleased her most of all, by reason of the rare skill she proved to have in it. The books that hazard had placed under her hand had extinguished her taste for reading.

She employed the rest of her time becoming bored over tapestry-work, when necessity did not oblige her to write a laconic letter to her mother.

The unique interest of her life, henceforth, was the future of her family. Without having any other sentiments for the members of that family than those of a lukewarm affection, she heaped them incessantly with testimonies of the keenest solicitude. It was no longer sufficient for her to affect to their wellbeing almost the entirety of the budget of her toilette, she never wearied of interceding with her husband in their favor, Maxwell gave without counting; anxious to second his wife's views, he delivered himself to the pleasure of according her even more than she asked of him. A third of his income sufficed for all his generosities. Irma's father and mother enjoyed an honest ease; among her brothers, the youngest were learning commerce, the others had founded costly establishments; her sisters, finally, generously endowed, could abandon themselves to the dream of an honorable marriage. Her ambition was fulfilled. There was only a maternal aunt, resident in Nevers, whose distress she had not had the consolation of being able to relieve.

In the presence of those results, however, she was no less melancholy and no less somber. It seemed that it was only important to her to ensure the calm of her conscience; not content only to see her family at long intervals, when circumstances demanded it, she also conserved, on those occasions, a cold and haughty exterior that repressed into the depths of their hearts the demonstrations of gratitude that were ready to burst forth.

Her isolation, moreover, was founded in reason. The baseness of her origin, as well as her husband's deplorable habits, closed to her the milieu where she might have been able, if not to please herself, at least to find a place. For want of being able to frequent her equals in fortune, she preferred to refuse all liaisons and live alone. Fundamentally, ennui was consuming her. Her glacial manners could have been compared to the layer of snow that sometimes covers the subterranean activity of a volcano.

Penetrated by the inanity of her forces, despairing of a fuller existence, she was nevertheless resigned, and had fallen gradually into a melancholy that, for her, was not without charm. The almost unanimous opinion of those in the vicinity who were aware of her apparent tastes, her eccentric humor and her savagery was that she did not have a very sound head. From the bourgeois, that opinion had spread to the peasants, and it was only the poor of whom she took care who did not attribute to her a somewhat deranged brain.

She struggled for many days before consenting to see the new guest at Les Ormes. John almost used violence in order to extract her from her retreat; he did not only feel the need to make others participate in the mad enthusiasm that the painter inspired in him; he also wanted, in the fear of his own insufficiency, Irma's beauty to serve to retain him at the château. Claude's praise never ceased to resound in the woman's ears, and the covetousness of the artist was incessantly stimulated by the husband's own words. So it can be affirmed that, morally, the latter threw his wife at the head of his friend Saint-Martin.

There can be no question of attenuating Irma's misdeeds; it is simply a matter of explaining them. The opportunity for her to exercise her keen penetration had always been lacking. Claude, served by the instinct that does not abandon even the most mediocre man in adventures of this sort, played next to her the role of a misanthrope overwhelmed by bitter disappointments, perpetually deceived in amity as in amour and tormented by the despair of ever finding a twin soul capable of understanding him. On top of that, not a word slid from his lips except to emphasize his merits or to recall his successes and the high destinies to which he ought to have been able to pretend. On the other hand, he affected to be repelled by Maxwell's vices, and applied himself incessantly to catch him *in flagrante delicto* in ignorance, in order to turn him to ridicule.

Could many women be found who, in the same conditions, would not be duped by those tactics? Irma did not adore her husband and, moreover, she was scornful of his penchants. In the eyes of his wife, John was further diminished and paled by the very reason of the magnified proportions and the glamour of the incomparable qualities of the artist. It would nevertheless be strangely absurd to apply the name of amour to Irma's sentiments. Claude paralyzed her by dint of maneuvering around her; it was the fascination of a snake exerted upon a bird. It is at least beyond doubt that the struggle was long and dolorous, and that the issue cost Irma her mental tranquility even while she did not believe herself to be shamefully scorned.

Furthermore, the cordial understanding was not one of long duration. Saint-Martin abhorred hindrance; as soon as he was assured of his triumph he took off his mask; from one day to the next the metamorphosis was complete. Irma wanted to believe, at first, that it was a comedy in poor taste, but temporary. It was necessary for her to render to the evidence. In a matter of a few hours, she learned more than the twenty-eight years of her age had taught her. The flash of enlightenment was no more prompt than her gaze. She penetrated the actor all the way to the most secret coverts of his nature, and quickly obtained the measure of that degraded man, devoid of conscience, heart and education, a slave to his vanity and capable of any baseness. Her shame was boundless and her dejection mortal. Saint-Martin was worth a thousand times less than her husband. Annihilated, after a fashion, by the weight of her error, she wondered how she could have been so culpable.

In the belief of a confirmed hypochondriac, however, the story would be quite simple. "The man," he says, "who conspires in the dishonor of his neighbor, only succeeds, most of the time, on condition of showing himself other than he is. As soon as he unmasks, judging the masquerade unnecessary, it almost always happens that he cannot sustain comparison even with the most execrated of men, and that is, for a woman who has not lost the sentiment of delicacy, incontrovertibly one of the harshest punishments of self-forgetfulness."

Saint-Martin believed himself to be doubly the master, on the one hand by virtue of amour and on the other by virtue of fear of scandal. He was deceived in both these previsions. The limits of his discernment scarcely permitted him to go beyond the appearances of that woman. She was impotent to content herself with a sentiment that her reason condemned, and possessed in addition a pride and an energy that put her beyond all dread. The vivacity of her scorn for Claude could only be compared with the ardor of her urgency to make him feel it.

He wanted to persist in a familiarity that he regarded as a privilege, but merely by the way that she looked at him, he was immediately reduced to silence and forced to respect. His vanity had been subjected to terrible proofs. Irma had not limited herself to heaping him with insults and defying him, she had also overtly disquieted her husband, until the day when he had decided to share her scorn and hatred. The painter's sojourn at the château importuned her; she could not even catch a glimpse of him without experiencing transports of anger; it was necessary for her to constrain him to depart. Her implacable resentment had promptly determined the result she desired with all the violence of passion.

She had learned that this very day was to illuminate the departure of her enemy, and her impatience to be rid of an odious proximity had woken her up at dawn. She was impatient to sense life around her, to hear the bustle of the domestics and the grating of wheels on the damp sand of the courtyard.

Her husband was ordinarily an early riser and he had the custom of supervising the work of the grooms personally; energetic oaths and the barking of dogs announced his presence in the vicinity of the stables. When seven o'clock chimed, however, nothing had stirred as yet. Irma was beginning to be alarmed and to fear that the departure, in consequence of some orgy, might be postponed until another day. Already, after having unbolted her bedroom door, she was raising her arm to ring for Justine, but a noise suspended her gesture.

Almost immediately, her door was violently pushed, and Maxwell suddenly introduced himself into the room.

VI

He was horribly pale, his red eyelids agape, so to speak; the disorder of his garments, soiled in places, testified sufficiently to the employment of his wakefulness. Something abnormal was happening within him, that was obvious; nevertheless, he was more reminiscent of a man under the weight of a mortification than that of an outrage; his fatigued features respired confusion rather than a spirit of vengeance. In his soul, in fact, the springs of which had been relaxed by debauchery, deep resentments were no longer possible; a few hours' sleep had sufficed to reduce his great fury to a simple sentiment of shame and bitterness. He even seemed rather troubled in his role of offended husband; a profound indecision was legible in his eyes and in his attitude.

Irma came to his aid. Impatient to know to what to attribute his matinal visit and his strange appearance, she demanded: "What's the matter with you? Aren't you leaving?"

"No," he replied, brutally. "I'm not leaving."

Turning his head away, however, he started measuring the room with an agitated stride. Irma followed him with her eyes for a few moments.

"Why?" she added, with an increasing astonishment.

John stopped two paces away from her and looked her in the eyes again.

"Hypocrite!" he said suddenly, with an expression bursting with scorn.

Irma's thought was so far from her husband's preoccupations that that insult turned her to stone. With an expression of amazement that was not feigned she demanded: "What are you saying?"

"I'm saying," John retorted, hotly, "that you might at least have arranged yourself in a manner to spare me so much ridicule."

"If you want me to understand," said Irma, impatiently, "speak more clearly."

"What!" cried John. "It's necessary that I learn from a strange mouth that your reserve is nothing but a comedy, that the modesty which, to my disorder, reddened your forehead, is only the mask of an ignoble libertinage!"

Irma no longer knew what to think; assurance disappeared from her features. Her husband added, in a bitter tone: "Truly, I thought I merited better than to become the laughing-stock of a man like that wretch Claude!"

Irma shuddered violently; her presence of mind almost abandoned her completely.

A hypothesis, more agile than lightning, shone within her and sustained her. Attaching to her husband one of those searching gazes under the fire of which it is impossible to lie, she said, audaciously: "Someone is playing with you. A neighbor, offended by my lack of warmth, or a domestic discontented by my rigidity, has decided to avenge himself by means of some malevolent insinuation."

"Go on," replied Maxwell, shaking his head with a sort of disdain.

"What appearance is there," Irma went on, recklessly, "that Claude has ever seriously occupied me? A man that I hate!"

"It hasn't always been thus."

"That's because I didn't know him," Irma retorted, with a somber and desperate expression. She added almost immediately, in her impatience to know the key to the enigma: "On what are you basing yourself, in sum, to throw that insult in my face?"

"On what am I basing myself?" Maxwell made a movement of indecision. "Hold on," he said, suddenly, "I pity you; don't betray yourself any further. You have no taste for lying, I know. I want to spare you the embarrassment of a shameful confusion."

"Well?" said Irma, breathless, decidedly emotional and fearful.

"Well," John added, "learn that I have the fact from your accomplice himself."

The shock that Irma received was so rude that she lost consciousness of her faculties momentarily. As she stepped back and sought the support of a table, her head inclined, a red cloud glided over her forehead, her eyeballs seemed to vitrify in their orbits; one might have taken her for a statue of horror.

The mirage of a doubt still brushed her mind.

"That's impossible," she said, in a faint voice. Then, raising her distressed face again in the direction of her husband, she added in a suppliant tone: "Come on, don't lie; tell me, without omitting any detail, what has happened."

Maxwell had the constancy to recount the previous evening's orgy, his quarrel with the painter, and finally, the strange confession that the other had thrown at him, sniggering.

No doubt was any longer possible.

Irma fell once again into her bleak dejection; she clenched her teeth; her inflated nostrils respired fury; a grim despair illuminated her eyes.

It required nothing less than the insulting reproaches of her husband to extract her from that dolorous torpor.

Maxwell said: "I saved you from opprobrium. Passing over your poverty as well as your origin, I made you my wife. You've feigned delicate tastes, you've heaped me with your scorn, you've gone so far as to forbid me entry to your bedroom. I've endured all that without complaint; your harshness seemed to me to be just. Better than that, whatever you've asked of me, you've never had to endure a single refusal on my part. How have you repaid me? With an abominable perfidy, in covering me with ridicule, in taking sides against me with a man I treated as a friend, who sat down at my table, who drew upon my purse unscrupulously."

While her husband was speaking, Irma emerged gradually from her torpor; the muscles of her face ceased to be rigid; the symptoms of active thought reappeared on her face and in her eyes.

However, she only heard her husband vaguely; her dolorous preoccupations prevailed over all the measures that the situation required.

By the manner in which she finally shook herself and raised her head, it was easy to comprehend that she had no more to reflect, and that her decision was made.

"Go on," she said, with a melancholy and despairing expression. "You cannot despise me more than I do myself."

"It's true, then!" cried John, whose credulous mind would have liked nothing better than to be deceived by a lie.

A long silence responded for Irma, who, from that moment on, no longer ceased to be worthy, and even in the enthusiastic confession of her husband, grand, superb and sublime.

"Don't ask me to explain to you how it happened," she added, "I don't understand it myself. It was a dream, a nightmare of folly, of vertigo. What do you expect? Under the empire of a hallucination, I seemed to see a magnificent, distinguished, powerful, superior man—more than a man, in sum. An execrable illusion, from which I awoke so unhappy! For, in the space of a lightning-flash, I no longer saw anything but a vulgar, cynical, debased being, inferior to the most brutal of your horse-dealers. From the species of admiration that he inspired in me, I passed almost without transition to scorn, disgust and horror. A poignant repentance gripped my soul. I cannot tell you how many days I remained annihilated under the weight of humiliation. Only the tyrannical need to see you share my repugnance and my hatred was able to triumph over that mortal depression. With what pleasure I would have seen you insult that man! With what passion I wanted to hear the carriage that would take him away from here. The secret of my fall was only known to the man who had dragged me into it, and I had the right to hope that he would carry that secret with him to the tomb. To your accusation of a little while ago, believing it to be the effect of a vague suspicion, I opposed an energetic denial. You have agreed yourself that I do not like lying, but your repose was well worth a lie. From the moment when you had drawn the truth from the very source, far from thinking of subterfuge, I am experiencing a kind of voluptuousness in discharging my soul of the burden that is crushing it, in confessing to you my sin, my repentance, my shame, my remorse and my torture."

Her musical, velvety contralto voice, which was exactly what one expected to hear from such as beautiful mouth, also borrowed from dolor the mysterious and penetrating charm that imagination lends to that of sirens.

Involuntarily, Maxwell was won over and inclined toward pardon.

The mocking shadow of Claude, which traversed his sight, deferred the expression of that charitable sentiment

"All that," he said, shaking his head, "doesn't prove very much."

"So you must realize," Irma said immediately, "that I cannot leave it at that."

"What do you mean?"

"If you had not been in the secret of my remorse," she replied, "it would have been possible for me, at length, not to blush in your presence. It is no longer the same today. I would like to look you in the face, but I cannot, even with twenty times more courage than I have. So I declare to you, and you can regard this declaration as irrevocable, that you are seeing me for the last time."

John made a gesture of astonishment.

"What do you intend to do?" he demanded. "No imprudence! Don't swear! Be assured, from now on, that I shall forget everything."

"But for myself," replied Irma, firmly, "it would never be in my power to forget anything; the memory will only be extinguished in me with life."

"Remember," said John, "that on my part the wrongs are numerous."

"Oh," said Irma, "your position is not comparable with mine. Your disorders cannot in any fashion authorize mine; you wouldn't believe that yourself for two days in succession. That is so absolutely true that at the first fit of ill-humor or anger, forgetting your good intentions, you would heap me with reproaches, perhaps insults."

"I'm ready to swear . . ."

"You know whether I am firm and resolute," Irma interrupted, in an energetic tone. "Despair has multiplied that firmness and resolution tenfold. Nothing in the world can deflect me from the resolution I have made."

"At least confide to me what your plan is," said Maxwell, anxiously.

Irma paused before replying; she appeared to be collecting herself.

"It's a fatal thing," she said, suddenly, raising her head. "Whatever you swear, you are seeing me for the last time . . ."

John tried to intervene again.

"Don't interrupt me," she added. "You don't know all my reasons. Before separating myself from you definitively, I have various things to tell you, several favors to ask of you. So sit down there and listen to me patiently, if that is possible . . ."

Maxwell, who had experienced his wife's indomitable energy many times, did not judge it appropriate to test it at that moment. To satisfy her, he sat down in the armchair that she designated to him, and waited.

VII

"According to you, you saved me from opprobrium," said Irma, after a pause. "No. What is exact is that you extracted me from a truly wretched condition. A curse seemed to weigh upon my father and my mother; they were sustaining in vain a desperate struggle against poverty, and were being extinguished prematurely in need, bitterness and chagrin. That isn't all; while, less resigned and less firm than me, my sisters were already thinking covertly about revolting against fortune and fleeing the paternal house, my brothers, still without profession, abandoned to themselves, reduced to envying the fate of others, might, under the constraint of necessity, have succumbed to a thousand temptations, resolving themselves to evil. Already, for me, the day was dawning when, impotent to ward off the peril, my soul devoured by anguish, I was witnessing the heartbreaking spectacle of the ruin, dishonor and despair of those who called me their daughter.

"Your generosity, John, changed that horrible future into a present full of wellbeing and consideration; thanks to you, my friend, that father and mother are living in ease, my sisters are assured against the hazards of tomorrow and my brothers are on the path to prosperity. All things considered, my dear John, with regard to the immense happiness that I owe you, far from reproaching you for your excesses, far from testifying scorn for you, far from rejecting you, I should, closing my eyes, perpetually kneeling before you, have kissed the dust on your feet, and adored you. For me you have been a Providence, a God . . .

"Try, then, at this moment when these verities are burning me, in which I sense all that with an inexpressible violence, in which gratitude is flooding from my soul, to measure my shame and my repentance, and understand, in sum, the point to which it would be impossible for me to live now in your presence. What! To you, my friend, so generous, so loyal, so brave, so noble, after all, I have been able to prefer for a day an hour, a second, a man already old, devoid of heart, intelligence, distinction and courage, a man whose entire body is not worth as much a single hair of your head! Oh, truly, it would be necessary that I had drunk all shame, that I had neither heart nor soul, that I were the least of wives, in order to be able henceforth, after such a crime, to look at you without blushing . . ."

In his modesty, Maxwell was far from believing that he merited so much praise. He was nevertheless charmed to hear such flattering words from Irma's mouth; his forehead was entirely serene, and his features no longer showed any trace of irritation against his wife.

To believe him, he asked for nothing but to pass a sponge over all bad memory and to recommence the honeymoon.

Irma was inflexible

"Let us speak now," she said, "about what I expect of you. I read the pardon in your eyes; that is not enough. It is not settled that my father, my mother, my sisters and my brother will no longer have need of you. One cannot foresee everything; an accident might soon happen. My brothers, in particular, do not seem to have been born under a lucky star. In spite of your liberalities, I have too often had to sustain them with money destined for my personal use. Finally, they are not sufficiently adept in business matters, and might at any moment feel the necessity of a helping hand. It's necessary that you give me your word, that you swear to me on all that you hold most sacred, not to abandon them, to come to their aid absolutely as if I were present to encourage you to do so. If you give me that word, as I know that you will not break it, I will owe it to you that I shall depart tranquil."

"With great heart," said John, emotionally, "I swear to you, whatever happens, to regard your family as mine, until my last day. But for the love of God, what does all this signify? Your resolution to quit me can't be serious. Where would you go?"

"Don't worry," replied Irma, with a bitter smile. "Let me thank you for the word you have given me. You are truly an excellent man; your generosity moves me to tears. It is necessary—necessary, you hear—for the good of my family, for the repose of all, that I do what I am doing. I cannot, even for a second, pass in your eyes for a schemer or an actress. It is important for me, above all, to reconquer your esteem and your affection. To whatever happens, say: 'It was written.' No human power, in fact, could prevent it. Keep silent, therefore; do not seek to know or to divine; limit yourself to granting me one last favor."

"What?" John asked.

"It is perhaps the most difficult thing I have to ask of you."

"Speak."

Irma hesitated.

"Speak," John repeated.

"It's a matter of sending here the man who has determined this scene between us, and leaving him alone with me for a few moments."

Maxwell did in fact, find that request strange

"What do you want with that poor devil?" he said scornfully.

"You shall know."

"Leave him to himself," said John. "Let him depart, and let there never again be any mention of him between us."

"Agreed; but before then, suffer that I see him. He might have the whim of recounting to others what he has confided to you. That cannot be. Render me this final service. Go and find him and bring him."

"You want him!" said Maxwell, indecisively.

"Dead or alive," retorted Irma, immediately.

"Well, so be it," said John, getting to his feet. He touched the door but retraced his steps

"But afterwards, at least," he said, considering his wife anxiously, "you'll consent to hear me. You do not know me very well, but you know that I am not without honor. Reflect that I am resolved to all the oaths that the repose of your future might require . . ."

With that, without even waiting for Irma's response, Maxwell went out precipitately.

VIII

Irma's room which measured an extent of about twenty paces, was as profound as it was wide and as high as it was profound. Two windows illuminated it; the battens of the door were facing them. Lilac wallpaper with darker flowers covered the walls, were a few engravings in monochrome, framed in gold, hung here and there. The armchairs, the chairs and stools, and the carpet underfoot, were the same hue as the walls. To the left, on entering, was the bed, which was embraced by muslin curtains like those at the windows; to the right was an elegant marble mantelpiece, ornamented with a pendulum clock, bronze cups, lamps and works of art, which stood out against the silvering of a magnificent mirror. Among the items of furniture, between the head of the bed and the wall, was a mahogany cupboard; in the diagonal corner there was a writing-desk; in the center a small table; in front of the left-hand window there was a large tapestry-work; finally, between the two widows, below a second mirror, there was a desk on which there was a large oval basket overflowing with wool of all colors.

In sum, that bedroom, the parquet of which had the polish of a mirror, the furniture of which was rich, where order was manifest, where nothing shocked the gaze, respired in its ensemble an unspeakable sadness.

Irma, meanwhile, rang loudly for her chambermaid. At least half an hour had gone by since Maxwell had gone out; it had been necessary for her to remain inactive for most of that time. At the foot of the bed, not far from the window, a dressing room opened into which she had penetrated as soon as she found herself alone. She had brought back therefrom a box in the form of a paint-box, which was nothing but the case of a pair of pistols.

Those weapons, of medium size, served for her favorite exercise. She had loaded them with bullets, fitted the percussion caps, and hidden them hastily, fully armed, in the basket, among the hanks of wool that filled it. It was quite impossible for that basket, drowned in the penumbra of the two windows, on the desk where one was habituated to see it, to awaken the slightest suspicion.

Having done that, Irma had got rid of the empty box. Then she had closed the window that she had opened when she got up, gone to the door, which she left ajar, rolled an armchair between the small table and the desk, sat down and waited, her eyes fixed on the clock.

Nearly twenty minutes had passed in that wait; no one came.

It was then that, doubtless griped by anxieties that are easy to comprehend, she had run to the side of her bed and had rung for Justine with a convulsive gesture.

The latter did not take long to show her face, becoming and joyful.

Irma did not even wait until she had come in. "Have you seen John?" she demanded, immediately

"Yes, Madame," replied Justine, advancing as far as the small table. "Just now he was running around the house from top to bottom."

"Why?"

"Looking for Monsieur Saint-Martin."

"Well?" said Irma, on the point of suffocating.

"Oh, Madame," the young woman replied, "the bird had flown the nest some time ago."

"What do you mean?" cried Irma. She opened her eyes immeasurably and clenched her fingers on the back of the armchair beside her.

Justine started to recount in detail what had happened. The story was inevitably curious. At daybreak, Pierre Maréchal, the château gamekeeper, surprised to hear someone opening a door from inside with precaution, had approached and had perceived Claude, charged with his valise, slipping outside stealthily. Pierre had questioned him about that clandestine departure. The painter had been in no hurry to reply. He had finally given the pretext of a rendezvous of the greatest importance that summoned him to town that very morning; his memory had only just reminded him of the date. He added that he feared missing the coach and had decided to go to wait for it to pass along the highway.

To a further observation from the gamekeeper, who affirmed that the vehicle would not go past for another two hours, at least, Claude had replied that it was important above all to go, that two hours would pass quickly, and that he would smoke his pipe while waiting. Pierre had accompanied him a third of the way along the avenue.

That departure, or rather that flight, had been all the more astonishing because he had heard his master give the order, the day before, to harness the carriage today for the town.

Irma listened to that story with a rare intensity of attention. Her pallor, her eyes full of somber flames, her clenched teeth and the convulsive movement of her hands all announced fever, ardor and devouring anguish in her.

"What has John done?" she asked, in an altered voice.

The young woman replied: "Monsieur gave the order to saddle a horse immediately. He's just departed.

From the windows at the front, Madame might still be able see him following the avenue, flat out."

Irma breathed more easily.

Nevertheless, her forehead only cleared to darken again immediately

"As long as he catches him!" she said, between clenched teeth, as if talking to herself.

Justine had heard. "Oh, don't worry, Madame," she said, "he'll catch up with him."

"At what time does the coach pass?"

"Nine o'clock."

Irma looked at the clock. "It's only eight," she said, with satisfaction.

Justine's keen attachment to her mistress, and the intimacy that solitude had inevitably established between the two of them, authorized the young woman to a great liberty of behavior and language. For the moment, she fixed bright eyes on Irma that were shining with curiosity and questions. Irma limited herself to confessing that Saint-Martin had said malevolent things about her, and that she intended to have an explanation with him.

"Have I told you," she said, shortly thereafter, with a view to directing Justine's attention elsewhere, "that I'm going to make a voyage?"

"Where to, Madam?"

"It's singular," said Irma, in a very simple tone. "I thought I'd told you about it. You're not unaware," she continued, "that I have an aunt in Nevers for whom I profess a great esteem. Well, against all expectation, John has consented that I go to see her."

"And Madame is departing . . . ?"

"Imminently," replied Irma. "My absence will doubtless be of rather long duration; it's probable that we won't see one another again for many days. While I think of it, I want to leave you a souvenir."

She took a ring from her finger in which a small emerald glittered, and put it on Justine's.

"You've often ecstasized about that ring," she said to her. "It pleases you; I'm giving it to you. Wear it in memory of me."

"Oh, how good Madame is!" exclaimed Justine, at the peak of delight. She admired the ring for a few seconds with a surge of joy, and added, sadly: "Madame isn't taking me with her? Is she not content with my service?"

"Yes indeed, my child," replied Irma, "but my aunt is poor; she probably only has very narrow accommodation; two people might inconvenience her."

The lie importuned Irma. She hastened to change the subject.

Apparently, her tranquility of mind was perfect. Justine, who had initially suspected something serious, was taken in; she was now entirely reassured.

"Now, my girl," said Irma, suddenly, "it's a matter of rendering me a small service."

The young woman lent an attentive ear.

Her mistress continued: "You're going to put yourself on sentry duty immediately at one of the first floor windows overlooking the avenue. As soon as you perceive my husband and Monsieur Claude, you'll run to inform me."

"Yes, Madame," said Justine heading for the door.

Irma stopped her with a gesture. "Take good care!" she said, sharply. "No distraction! Remember that you'll disoblige me profoundly if you quit your post, even for a minute, or a second."

"Have no fear Madame," said Justine, slipping away with the lightness of a goat-kid.

Irma still had a few moments before her. Those instants were entirely devoted to her family, as it was easy to observe subsequently. On one of the shelves of her cupboard, a group of little boxes was discovered, at the bottom of each of which one or more of her jewels lay. On one of those boxes was read: *To my sister Louise*, on the next, *To my sister Léontine*, and so on.

She had divided up the whole of her jewel-case in that manner. Her mother and her aunt, her sisters and her brothers, had one last pledge of her affectionate attention.

Not far from those various legacies a letter was found whose address bore the name of John Maxwell. That letter was written in a firm hand, and thus drafted:

My husband will not refuse to see to it that each of the boxes arranged on this shelf will be handed to its addressee. He will also permit that my sisters divide my linen, my dresses and all the other objects of toilette that belonged to me. I am avenging myself for him for more than for me. He would not only be ridiculed, he would soon be thought cowardly if the filthy creature who spat the secret of my shame in his face lived. That cannot be; it shall not be. My repentance, of which I am giving him the measure, might perhaps render my memory dear to him. Let him prove that to me by making a law of the things he has sworn to me.

Irma.

The material time was lacking for her to write a longer testament. Justine suddenly opened the door and, out of breath, penetrated into the room.

"Madame! Madame!" she cried. "I can see someone at the end of the avenue; it seems to me that it's Monsieur John and Monsieur Saint-Martin."

"Let's see!" said Irma, resolutely.

She went to her writing-desk, took out a little telescope and marched on the young woman's heels.

The latter had divined accurately.

Armed with her telescope, Irma could see distinctly, at a fairly long distance, her husband, on horseback, and Claude walking alongside him.

"That's good," said Irma, leaving the spot and the room. Having reached the corridor that led to her own room, she said to Justine, who had followed her: "Actually, I don't need you any more. You can go down to the kitchen, and don't come out again until I ring for you. It's understood that you mustn't open your mouth about all this to anyone." She paused, and then added, in a soft tone: "Go, my girl, and do as I ask, if you have a veritable affection for me."

240

"Oh, Madame!" cried Justine, precipitating herself upon Irma's hand and kissing it. "If I love you!"

"Go, my child, go," repeated Irma wiping away a tear.

She went back into her room; at the same time, Justine went downstairs.

IX

When he quit his wife, Maxwell was animated by a prodigious overexcitement. Proud of that woman, intoxicated by her eulogies, flattering himself that he would make her renounce her projects, he was burning to serve her as she wished—which is to say, as a slave. Irma's inflexible determination to see the painter only alarmed John moderately; he found it natural enough that she would want to reproach Claude for his odious behavior. As for what she proposed to do thereafter, John's mind was too superficial to foresee what implacable resentments might impel a wife such as his to do. In his view, Irma had simply made a resolution no longer to live with him. In that case, might she not render to the evidence of his devotion, his surges of passion and fanaticism? His anxieties on that subject were, therefore, soon calmed. Exclusively preoccupied with getting his hands on Claude, he ran up the stairway that led to his former friend's room.

The room was deserted.

The painter had also cleared it of everything that belonged to him.

John searched the house from top to bottom. Then he ran to the stables and questioned the domestics. Pierre Maréchal edified him immediately on what he desired to know. At that news, John gave the order to saddle a horse; in the grip of the feverish ardor of a hunter in pursuit of game, he helped with the task himself. A few moments later, under the action of the spur and the crop, the horse was flying like an arrow between the poplars of the avenue.

The completely unexpected anger of Maxwell, in the midst of drunkenness, had removed the scales from the miniaturist's eyes; grave apprehensions had pursued him in sleep and had divided his slumber with all sorts of bad dreams. The fumes of the wine had scarcely ceased to weigh upon his senses when he awoke. At the sight of John, who was snoring on the floor beside him, the glasses and the broken bottles, and the disorder of the room, it required little mental effort to recall the details of the previous evening's scene. A great anxiety took hold of him. Rapidly enlightened as to the extent of his incredible treason, he sat up and then stood up, as if struck by a kind of panic.

His long habitude of Maxwell doubtless spared him the shame of fearing him; nevertheless, Maxwell was not a man to keep the secret of his misfortune to himself; it was a sure bet that, when he awoke, his first concern would be to go to his wife's room and burst out in insults. Bad judge of others as he was, Claude could not be entirely mistaken abut Irma; she had proved to him her savage energy and vindictive spirit, her impotence to pardon an outrage. At any rate, that woman had always imposed on him, always frightened him.

Without glimpsing how she might avenge herself, the wretch, full of the sentiment of his error, had at least to fear merited reproaches, threats and a violent scene. Scandal might fill the château without compensating any damage. Better to flee. In the eyes of the guilty party, the wisdom of that measure was obvious. At her husband's accusation, Irma's first impulse would doubtless be to deny it energetically, and the second to invoke the testimony of Claude himself. A search would be made for the latter; his disappearance, arming John with the pretext to believe in an imposture, would probably have the result of calming him down.

Reassured somewhat by that plan, the painter, on whom the atmosphere of the château weighed like lead in any case, slipped out of the room cautiously, went up to his room, packed his valise hastily and went downstairs on tiptoe, holding his breath. It was then that he had encountered the gamekeeper and had exchanged with him the conversation related by Justine.

Reduced to floundering in the wet sand, Claude could not walk very rapidly; he took at least an hour to travel the length of the avenue. The oppression that gripped his heart diminished a little, but he only recovered the courage to rest and light his pipe when he reached the gate of the château. He was, however, far from having a tranquil soul; his preoccupations were so intense that he let his pipe go out twice for want of thinking about it. His sense of security would evidently only be reborn on the banquettes of the coach that would carry him toward the town. In the meantime, the tree-trunk on which he was sitting did not appear to him to be far enough away from the place from which he had emerged. In spite of his profound hypotheses, what if one or other of his hosts had the whim of pursuing him?

Solicited by black presentiments not to pause for any longer, the thought tempted him of going as far as the neighboring village and waiting in the tavern for the passage of the coach, but the distance measured at least eight kilometers, and, not to mention that he only had bad legs and was charged with a heavy valise, he already felt harassed by fatigue. Nevertheless, as the minutes went by the place seemed less and less safe. The dread of seeing the husband or the wife appear at the bend of the path did not leave him an instant's repose.

He finally decided to move away from the gate and at least sit down in a place where he would not have to fear apparitions. About five hundred paces from the avenue, at the foot of a tall tree, a place carpeted with grass, to which he limped, appeared to him to be a precious observatory. Not only did his gaze extend a long way along the road from that height, but a dense bush growing behind the tree was entirely favorable, in the event that a prompt retreat became necessary.

Unfortunately, in his prudence, he counted without the invincible slumber that did not take long to close his eyes. The sound of a horse galloping over the pavement snatched him abruptly from his lethargy. He lifted his eyelids with difficulty, and then widened them enormously and shivered at the sight of Maxwell advancing like a hurricane in his direction.

With one bound, Claude was on his feet; immediately, instinct pressed him to flee, but it was too late. John, whose piercing eyesight he had not escaped, was already slowing the pace of his horse.

The painter possessed a thick cane without which he never walked; he clutched it in his hand instinctively and awaited his adversary with a firm footing and a resolute air.

Meanwhile, Maxwell stopped his foam-flecked horse, dismounted and came tranquilly toward the fugitive.

"Why," he asked, with an ironic expression, "are you putting yourself on the defensive like that? Do you imagine that I'm going to attack you?"

Saint-Martin allowed some shame to show. "Your haste in pursuing me," he said, "so closely resembles a threat."

"You're in error," John replied, with a more marked hint of irony. "I wanted, more than anything, to make you party to the high idea that your flight gives me of your courage."

"Bah!" said Claude, in a disengaged tone. "Where was the urgency in awaiting your awakening? Yesterday, when we were drunk, you drew an absurd confidence from me. Henceforth, we can no longer look one another in the face. A struggle between us, or at least a painful quarrel, was inevitable. I wanted to spare us the regret of that. In your interest, even more than mine, it seemed wise to disappear. Let me tell you that you were wrong to refuse to understand and not to stay at home. The best thing for you to do, in fact, is to forget what I said. Don't have the ridiculous idea of talking about the adventure. You can still suppose that I have calumniated your wife; I don't oppose that. It might be the case, after all. It remains for me to express my repentance; believe in it, and let's quit one another, if not mutually animated by the amity of old, at least without anger and without rancor."

Maxwell enjoyed the humiliating confusion of the painter with a kind of sensuality, and enveloped him with a gaze dripping with scorn. After having satisfied himself amply on that point, he composed himself with a glacial expression.

"I have nothing against you," he said, laconically. "I can even affirm that, with regard to myself, the idea would never have occurred to me of hindering your retreat . . . but," he resumed, after a pause, "my wife wants to see you; she begged me insistently to bring you to her, and I'm in haste to enter into a campaign to please her."

"What does she want of me?" asked Saint-Martin.

"I don't know."

"Doubtless to heap me with reproaches," he continued, "to constrain me to a lie. What would be the point, since I authorize you to certify her that I confess my sins and repent? Would it not be absurd, after that, for me to go to as futile scene, as disagreeable for her as for me? I won't go."

"What?" said John.

"I won't go." the painter repeated.

"We'll see about that," said Maxwell.

"You evidently can't force me," Claude added, "to go where I don't want to go."

"I beg your pardon," said John, whose cold and firm attitude really had something redoubtable. "You don't know me at all. Until now it has pleased you to regard me as a coward and treat me as such. You haven't perceived that my pretended weakness was only condescension for your person. From that results the grave error of believing in your ability to make me tremble. It might cost you greatly to persevere any longer in that illusion. I have sworn to my wife to bring you before her dead or alive, and I warn you that I shall do as I have sworn to do. You will therefore consent to follow me politely, unless you prefer to fight here and now, with any weapons that come to hand."

Shaken as much as surprised by an energy of which he had not even suspected the existence, Claude judged it appropriate to lower the tone.

"Ah!" he said. "You doubtless don't sense that your threats are insulting for me? I want to forget them, but in return, be sage, retrace your steps and, trust me, say that you were unable to catch up with me."

"Let's go!" said Maxwell shrugging his shoulders. "I only have one word; in my eyes, every oath is sacred. Pick up your bag and follow me."

"I shall certainly do no such thing."

"In truth, no such thing?" said John. "Oh, my dear Monsieur, decidedly, I'm beginning to doubt your bravery. What! You, the bravest of the brave, the vanquisher of vanquishers, are recoiling, with every appearance of being afraid of a feeble woman?"

The painter lost patience when John added: "Are you not, truly, as I supposed, nothing but a braggart and a coward?"

"Not one word more!" he cried angrily.

"Well, personally," retorted Maxwell, whose voice rose to the pitch of violence, "I declare that if you don't consent to follow me immediately, without any more reflections, I shall take you for the most despicable and vilest of rogues and I shall strike you down here and now with the handle of this riding-crop."

The measure was full; Claude could not endure any more. Bounding, after a fashion, under the wound, he lifted his valise abruptly on to his shoulders and said, resolutely: "Let's go."

John got back into the saddle and followed him.

During the trajectory, relatively long, which they made side by side, neither of them thought of breaking the silence. They both seemed prey to the gravest preoccupations.

To see Saint-Martin, his head bowed and worried, advancing with a limp, under the escort of Maxwell on horseback, one would truly have thought him a malefactor being conducted to prison by the gendarmerie.

They arrived thus at the foot of the château. Maxwell dismounted and said to the painter in a low voice, with an attitude full of significance: "Go up to the first floor and go to my wife's room, where she is waiting for you. After that, you'll be free."

"That won't take long!" retorted Claude, who went in with the urgent expression of a man in haste to finish promptly.

In the meantime, John confided his horse to the hands of a domestic and patiently stood sentinel before the door to the ground floor.

X

Heavy clouds of a uniform hue still masked the sky; the daylight continued to be somber, the air cold. In the surrounding area, the trees, which designed dazzling tableaux for the eyes with their autumnal tints, as vivid as they were varied, no longer associated their desolate and tarnished foliage with anything but perspectives of a distressing melancholy.

It is a notorious fact that, in the effective dramas that frighten our planet, exterior nature almost always seems to be curiously in harmony with action. The numerous domestic staff of the château, whose coming-and-going and chatter ordinarily animated the environment, seemed to have been given the word to remain hidden and silent. Apart from Maxwell, on sentry duty before the door, no one gave any sign of life. One could have believed that the house was deserted.

Irma was alone on the first floor. The silence that enveloped the château permitted her to hear distinctly every one of the footsteps of the man for whom she was waiting. Her sang-froid, at the beginning of the scene, proved the extent to which she feared alarming her enemy and putting him to flight. She was positioned in the middle of the room, sitting in an armchair, her gaze fixed on the door. Saint-Martin was now approaching with an irresolute tread. The urgency that he had shown in the threshold of the ground floor appeared to have cooled considerably.

He decided, however, to push the door, which stood ajar, and to take a step into the room. His habitual audacity disappeared under the most incontestable confusion.

"Come in, then," said Irma, in an almost caressant voice, without quitting the armchair. "I have to talk to you."

Claude still hesitated. With her affected calm and her quiet manner, Irma frightened him. He would have much preferred to see her furious and bursting forth with reproaches.

"Are you afraid of me?" she added, with a slight tone of mockery. "Why? You've made a blunder; it's a matter of repairing it. I need, for that, to reach an understanding with you. Come on," she continued, impatient because the painter did not budge, "close that door, turn the key in the lock, draw the bolts and come and sit down here, in this armchair." As she spoke, Irma had risen to her feet and had rolled the armchair toward the desk, three paces from the basket.

She had never shown a more affable face or more engaging manners.

Claude fell into the infernal trap that she had set for him; his vanity made him believe immediately in those conciliating words; he imagined that Irma regretted having offended him, that she was afraid of him, and was asking for mercy. What fortified him further in that imagination was that, darting his suspicious gaze around him, he only perceived in the room what he had always seen there.

As prompt to reassure himself as he was to alarm himself, he closed and locked the door, shot the bolts, and turned toward Irma with a sort of amorous haste.

In the meantime, suddenly ceasing to smile, mute, doubtless oppressed by sensing the enemy in her power, Irma indicated the armchair to him with her hand, and as he approached it, she moved backwards toward the desk and reached toward the basket.

Saint-Martin, although surprised to see her visibly changed, did not augur anything suspect in that maneuver; he placed his valise and his hat on the small table and sat down.

Three paces away from him, standing up, Irma had her back turned to the mirror and her hands resting on the desk.

As if idly, she slid her right hand behind her as far as the basket and gradually plunged her hand into it.

Claude gazed at her without suspicion.

They remained in that respective attitude for a few seconds, observing one another.

Irma, her right hand drowned in the wool in the basket, which she was masking with her body, seemed made of stone.

Gradually, by dint of looking at her enemy, the blood withdrew from her cheeks; her entire face contracted horribly, and a blaze was ignited in her eyes.

The painter no longer knew what to think.

Suddenly, she exploded like a mine.

"Wretch!" she spat, between her teeth, in a tone of indignation and hatred. "What have you done?"

Saint-Martin shuddered, and considered Irma with stupor. "Oh well," he said, after a pause. "If that's why you had me come . . ."

"Why would I have made you come," Irma retorted, vehemently, "if not to mark my hatred and crush you with my scorn?"

Claude became very pale. Nevertheless, not comprehending that he had anything to fear from a lone woman, he promptly reassured himself and made the decision to stand up to the scorn audaciously

"Your hated and your scorn," he said cynically "are only words, which slide over me like water over a duck. If you believe me, you'll spare me reproaches and put the big words to one side. Better to occupy ourselves without delay with poor John."

"What are you daring to say?" Irma interjected, with a thunderous expression. "Don't you understand that my torture is that of having preferred to him, by surprise, for the duration of a lightning-flash, a monster of imbecility, an ignoble braggart of vices?"

"Ah! Ah!" said Saint-Martin, turning impatiently to the right and left, losing all his assurance before the reckless transport of the woman.

"If only I had your privileges," she continued, with a sort of fury, "I would slap you, I would spit in your face, and I would oblige you to an implacable fight. You have offended me mortally, you have rendered life impossible for me; I do not want you to do that with impunity!"

The painter, decidedly frightened, was tempted to flee.

Irma, her eyes glittering, struck him with a sort of paralysis.

At the same time, with a gesture as rapid as thought, she threw her right hand forward, armed with a pistol.

A shot resounded, which shook the entire house.

Saint-Martin, hit in the face, collapsed against the back of the armchair.

Four or five seconds later, a second shot burst forth with no less noise, and Irma fell to the floor, her breast traversed by a bullet.

At the two gunshots, which struck his ears almost simultaneously, Maxwell, who was commencing to be gained by impatience and anxiety, shuddered with alarm. Bewildered, he ran into the house and ran up to the first floor crying:

"Help! To me, my friends! Irma! Irma!"

From the kitchen and the stables the domestics came running and followed him closely. Soon, for the most part, they were grouped around John, who, exhausting his strength trying to break down his wife's door, never ceased shouting in an unspeakable accent of terror: "Irma! Irma!"

Finally, he appealed to the most robust of those surrounding him. "My friends," he said to them, in a pleading one, "help me to break down this door . . . Irma! What's happened . . . ? You heard . . ."

The door resisted all the efforts of the domestics. Pierre then ran downstairs and soon came back armed with a crowbar.

Shortly afterwards, through the debris of the door, Maxwell and the domestics precipitated into the room.

A frightful scene chilled them to the bone.

Not far from Claude, collapsed in the armchair, whose bloody head was tilted over his shoulder, Irma lay in the middle of a pool of blood. She was livid; her contracted face still expressed a savage energy; in spite of the frightful fixity of her gaze, the flames that had previously shone in her eyes were not completely extinct. Her hand, under the violent and irresistible action of the muscles, had thrown away the weapon with which she had shot herself. The bullet, it was established later, had traversed the heart; Irma must have died instantly.

Gripped by an inexpressible despair, John threw himself upon her and took her head in his hands.

"Irma! My poor Irma!" he cried, dissolving in tears and covering her with kisses.

Apart from Justine, who, mad with terror, had run out of the room uttering heart-rending screams, and Pierre Maréchal, who, better advised, went down to the stables, harnessed a horse and went to fetch a physician, the other domestics watched the scene open-mouthed.

John, animated by a tender passion, transported his wife to the bed. Only then did he turn round and, his eyes full of scorn and hatred, occupy himself with Saint-Martin. The latter had received the bullet full in the face, beneath the right eyebrow; it had penetrated the cavity of the eye and expelled the eyeball, which was dangling over the cheek. It was judged that he too had ceased to live.

The surgeon, who soon arrived, did not share that opinion. Although poor Irma really was nothing more than a cadaver, Claude was still breathing. A probe aided the surgeon to discover that the bullet, after having expelled the eye from the orbit, had lodged in the jaw. The painter also had a wound in his right hand. It was supposed that as the shot was fired, he had instinctively raised that hand and had placed it between the weapon and his head. He was transported provisionally to a room in the château, where the surgeon, seconded by a physician, came to visit him every day.

The event had an enormous resonance in the area, within a circumference whose radius grew incessantly. An investigation was opened by the law. It was only able to speak in memory; it ended with the conclusion of a double murder, the author of which no longer existed.

Irma was buried with extraordinary pomp. Only then did innumerable remarks burst forth in her praise. Twenty mouths opened to proclaim that her generosity was inexhaustible, that no one had ever implored her in vain, that it was necessary to renounce counting how many times she had come to the aid of discreet misfortunes. It was found, in sum, that all those who had known her had esteemed and loved her. A considerable crowd, in the midst of which women in tears were observed, notably Justine, whose sobs redoubled with every step, followed her hearse as far as the village cemetery, where Maxwell had erected, at great expense, a tomb that was more sumptuous than elegant.

The truth about the death was already circulating among the people who accompanied her to her final dwelling. A country-dweller pronounced naïvely this funeral oration: "The most beautiful thing about that woman's life was her death."

Saint-Martin survived the catastrophe. One might be tempted to see, in that providential salvation, proof that talion, in human hands, is only a specious right. Claude, however, had one of his eye-sockets empty, his face disfigured by a terrible wound that marked him like a stigma.

As for John Maxwell, in whose eyes time embellished Irma more and more, he was always to act with his wife's family in a manner that testified that he professed, at least, the religion of the oath.

Appendix:

The Deaf

SOME distance from the village where his house was, on the edge of the highway, in a solitary spot bordered to the right and left by dense woodland, a worthy man was guarding a hundred sheep that belonged to him.

That worthy man was deaf.

By his appetite, he sensed that the hour of supper had sounded some time ago, and from one moment to the next he raged more energetically against his wife, who had not brought him anything to eat.

Only his sheep prevented him from running to the village.

This was what he finally decided to do.

On the same side of the road, fifty or sixty paces further on, an old woman was cutting grass for her cow. The old woman in question was curbed simultaneously by age and the weight of a detestable reputation. In spite of those well-known details, our man, pressed by hunger, did not hesitate. He went to that woman.

"Would you be kind enough," he said to her, "to keep an eye on my sheep while I go to have a meal?

When I return, we'll see. I'll give you a recompense that will give you reason, I hope, to be satisfied."

The old woman was also deaf.

"What do you want with me?" she retorted, bitterly. "The grass in this ditch belongs to me as to everyone else; what right do you have to prevent me from cutting it? What are you thinking? Apparently I ought to let my cow die in order for your sheep to have a few more mouthfuls! In what times are we living? Leave me alone! Go the Devil!"

The shepherd mistook the gesture with which the old woman accompanied that abuse for a mark of consent. Without another word, he turned away and walked rapidly toward his domicile. His wife's forgetfulness appeared to him to be inexcusable, and his impatience to chastise her accelerated his pace.

At the scene that awaited him, his anger turned to pity. His wife was ill. Having eaten poisonous mushrooms, she was writhing on the floor in terrible agony.

Our man picked her up and, by means of intelligent care, succeeded in neutralizing the effects of the poison. Then he hastened to have his meal, and hurried back to the place where he had left his sheep.

Briskly as he had acted, his absence had lasted more than an hour. His anxieties were all the sharper because of the evil renown of the witch under whose safeguard he had left the flock. Scarcely had he returned than he cast a suspicious gaze in the direction of the old woman and checked to see whether any of his sheep might be missing. The count was complete; he was delighted.

That's what prejudice does, he thought. *There's a poor old woman to whom thefts are imputed every day, and who is probably a perfectly honest woman. Let's forbid ourselves such prejudices and recompense her by reason of the wrong that malicious gossip has done her. After that, if she really does have commerce with the Devil, well, perhaps my generosity will put out of her mind forever the idea of putting a spell on me . . .*

His gaze then fell upon a large, fat ewe that only had one fault, that of being lame. That infirmity only reduced its value slightly. He took it in his arms and went to the old woman, put the animal at her feet and said, while designating it with his hands:

"This is to recognize the service you've rendered me, my worthy woman. Deign to accept this ewe as a present."

The old woman reared up like an angry cock. Casting her eyes on the ewe and perceiving that it was lame, she replied with vivacity: "Holy dolors, this is new! What does this signify? May God abandon me if I stirred from this place in your absence! How dare you accuse me of casting a spell on that animal and taking pleasure in breaking its foot? You must be possessed! I didn't expect this: arms falling upon me!"

"Its wool is fine and silky," the worthy man added, "the flesh is excellent. If you don't want to regale yourself with it, you can sell it for a good price."

"And I repeat," cried the harridan, furiously, "that I haven't even made a movement toward your sheep! You're a rogue, an impious impostor. Go away! Get away from me, or I'll scratch your eyes out with my old fingernails."

She was menacing; one of her hands was gripping a billhook convulsively, the other extending its redoubtable fingernails.

Amazed at first, and then frightened, the man threw himself backwards and raised his staff instinctively. That purely defensive gesture finished exasperating the old woman. She unleashed insults at him, and looked at if she wanted to put out his eyes. He fell prey himself to a muted irritation; patience escaped him. The staff and the billhook were about to collide . . .

At the same moment, a horseman, stimulating his mount with hands and feet, was advancing toward the two adversaries with the bridle down. They perceived him. Immediately forgetting to fight, they both barred the road and forced the rider to stop. While the old woman took hold of the bridle to the right, the shepherd seized the one to the right, and, addressing the rider, said very politely:

"I beg you, Monsieur Cavalier, to be the judge between this woman and me. She has rendered me a small service. I hastened to recognize it by offering her a ewe. Well, not content to abuse me, she is also threatening me with a billhook."

For her part, the old woman cried:

"Don't listen to him! He's lying! It's not my fault that one of his ewes is lame. The bumpkin wasn't watching them. In his absence, I never ceased cutting grass, at least a hundred paces away from the flock . . ."

Things could not have worked out more unfortunately. The horseman was no less hard of hearing than the people who were speaking to him. Moreover, his pale physiognomy respired anxiety and dread.

"Yes, I confess," he said, in a distraught voice, "this horse doesn't belong to me. Refrain, however, from seeing me as a thief. I'm in a great hurry; a horse happened to be at hand; it had no master, and I mounted it in order to go more rapidly. That's the whole truth. Is it yours? Take it and let me pass, for, word of honor, I don't have a moment to lose . . ."

For want of hearing, the old woman imagined that the horseman was taking the side of the shepherd, and the latter that the rider was supporting the old woman. In consequence, they started abusing one another again, threatening one another vehemently and reproaching the man they had taken as an arbiter for his partiality and injustice. For his part, the rider, supposing that those furious individuals were arguing with him and showing him their fists because of the horse he had taken, he mingled his voice with the concert of recriminations and insults . . .

All three of them then remarked an old man who, head bowed, was coming along the road, and who was going past them without even turning his head. A man of that age and that gravity seemed to them to unite all the conditions of an excellent judge. They ran to him and begged him to grant them a minute's audience. Meanwhile, each of them, all three in chorus, exposed their grievances and invited him to decide which of them was right, against the other two . . .

It is scarcely believable, but the old man was even more deaf than they were.

He replied: "Yes, yes, I hear you. It's my wife who sent you, isn't it? She's induced you to oppose my departure; you want to convince me that I ought to return to her. Don't think of it. My resolution is unshakable. Some time ago, I abstracted myself from the austerities of the cloister in order to savor the pretended pleasures of marriage. Heaven has chastised me cruelly. Do you know my wife well, my friends? She's a veritable demon; Xantippe would have seemed an angel by comparison. It isn't possible for me to live another day with such a malevolent creature. She has made me commit more sins than two hundred years of hard penance can efface. I'm going on a pilgrimage to Rome. My intention is to hide in some convent and to try, by means of fasting and prayer, to obtain remission for my faults. After that, I'm determined to travel the world with a sack on my back and to beg for my bread. All woes seem preferable to me than being alone with the woman I'm fleeing . . ."

What the old man was saying did not inhibit the others from speaking in the slightest. It seemed to them that the old man was procrastinating and lacked the courage to state his opinion. One pressed him to finish; another accused him of weakness; the old woman called him a driveller, and the old man begged them to leave him alone. A century of such explanations would not have served to put them in accord.

While all four of them were shouting loudly, without being able to make themselves heard, the horseman saw people in the distance who were advancing at a rapid pace. Under the influence of a troubled conscience, imagining that he was dealing this time with gendarmes, he dismounted briskly from the horse and ran away as fast as he could.

Other motives decided the shepherd to quit the party. His flock had strayed and drawn away considerably. He hastened to catch up with them. The accidents and contradictions of the day filled him with a somber sadness. As he went, he cursed the arbiters and deplored bitterly that justice had disappeared from the world.

Although still exasperated, the old woman returned to her pile of grass. Not far away, the lame ewe was grazing tranquilly. She seized it, put a cord around its neck, and, in order to avenge herself on its master for his unjust accusation, took it home with her.

As for the old man, he continued his route as far as the next village and stopped there in order to spend the night. Repose and sleep tempered his ill-humor against his wife considerably. Relatives and friends, learning of his flight, had set forth on his tracks and soon caught up with him. They finished calming him down and persuaded him to retrace his steps, promising to employ all their influence in reducing his wife to mildness and submission.